CW01432451

To

Edith

Bar wish

Sam x

ISBN 978-9550780-5-7

First edition

Published 2007 by Pioneer Readers
AN IMPRINT OF FYGLEAVES LTD
FYG STUDIO, WEST EALING, UK W13 9JR
www.pioneer-readers.org   www.fygleaves.co.uk
COVER: WILLIAM RUSSELL © FYGLEAVES LTD
FRONT COVER PHOTOGRAPHY BY MATTHEW EMMOTT
BACK COVER PHOTOGRAPHY BY WILLIAM RUSSELL
PRINTED AND BOUND BY CPI ANTONY ROWE

Samantha Priestley

Despite Losing it on Finkle Street

fygleaves PUBLISHING

Acknowledgements

Tom, Eva and Lily;
Dan; Kieron; and Barry for the house at Hilltop.

The police car tagged the ambulance all the way to the village. There wasn't much call for them out here in the silent hills. Normally their attention was pulled greedily to the more populated areas of Keswick and Cockermouth, sometimes Windermere.

The older of the two policemen hated anything involving death: he was probably in the wrong job really. His partner watched him. Could feel his nervousness, his jaw set tight as his gloved hands sheathed the wheel. Young people, middle-aged people, old people, it didn't matter: he said death always made him think of his own kids, and the frailty of life.

"It gets to you," he said. "When you've got kids. Life just becomes more precious somehow."

But the younger policeman, still childless, said that was nonsense. Whether you had children of your own or not you could always feel the cold blunt end of a death. The worst thing was having to look into a relative's eyes and see that what you had to tell them was so impossible it stopped time, it defied everything. And no matter how old the person had been, there was always something momentous about life coming to an end.

"It's the only certainty," he told his partner. "Especially in our line of work."

They already knew this was another death. And the younger policeman knew he was always the one who had to do the dirty jobs, always the one who had to deal with sadness.

The ambulance in front of them slowed as it approached the village, its wheels turning mournfully in respect; its mute sirens useless now and cold above their heads. The policemen followed until they stopped behind the ambulance and turned off the engine. This was what they were paid for.

"Come on," the younger officer said. "Let's get it over with."

*

This was probably the loneliest place on earth right now. And that wasn't what Rachel had expected. She took off her coat and laid it on a barstool. Hitched her shoulder bag back over her arm as it repeatedly fell forward. The pub was dark inside. It smelled of stale beer and Rachel could see a wet patch on the carpet where someone had already spilled a drink. She wondered for a moment what she was doing here.

She'd promised herself at work that she wouldn't cry today: she knew her boss was useless with anything like that, and it was almost as if he resented her having the previous day off for the funeral. Even for someone so close to her. But while he was out for his lunch a simple memory brought back a tear.

A girl from the bakery was browsing quietly in the shop at the time and gently put a hand to Rachel's elbow, asking if she was all right.

"It's fine, thank you," Rachel said. "It's just…" she could hardly make the words happen. Did that mean she hadn't come to terms with it yet?

"It's OK," the girl said. "You don't have to tell me what it is…" Then a smile brightened the girl's face and she said, "Listen, me and some of the others from the shops are going for a drink after work tonight. Not for long, just the pub over the road. Why don't you come with us?"

Rachel felt better; she thought it was the only genuine piece of kindness she'd received in these past couple of days.

She went straight over to the pub at 5.30. The girl from the bakery was standing there by the bar with about six others, all still wearing uniforms with name tags pinned to their breasts. She said hello to Rachel and introduced her around the small crowd. But within five minutes they were talking amongst themselves, the ease of previous conversations and an old intimacy binding them together. No one really knew Rachel here, and no one talked to her much after that. Standing in the pub, Rachel felt hopelessly out of place. She was forced to buy drinks to gain attention. Slinking up to the other girls, feeling like a fraud.

In the village everyone knew her, but there was too much sympathy. Only now, sitting on her own, did she realise how powerful, how meaningful, every close death can be. She didn't want sympathy, and she didn't want her own thoughts to be the only ones echoing around her head. Death was in the local newspapers again this week, as it always was, but it was different today. This time it had taken someone so close to her.

What was it she wanted? Company, not sympathy. A new start. Although she hadn't come here to drown her sorrows, she now took a long sip of her Bacardi and coke and realised she had just emptied her third glass in one gulp.

So she lined up a row of drinks for the girls from the bakery and the café, in the hope that they wouldn't leave her there alone. Maybe they'd even let her join in with their jokes, their tireless laughing. She stayed close to them while they drank.

Rachel tilted her body towards the others, trying to feel their warmth, trying to catch some of it for herself. Like a virus, she thought. Could happiness be infectious like that? Could Rachel feel it rub from their bodies onto hers? Could she be like these women?

Rachel told herself that this was the place she shouldn't feel lonely. At least there were always people in the pub, always voices, bodies, smiles and eyes. But now they too were talking about a death, gossiping about the headlines in the paper. The last thing she wanted to talk about.

She had known she would miss her when she died, but she hadn't counted on the loneliness. Hadn't realised she would feel quite like this. It was even worse that her neighbours had wanted to blame her; even though the police didn't see it that way.

She was the one who would miss her gran the most. She was missing her more than she expected.

*

This was probably the loneliest place on earth right now.

It was forsaken and desolate place. A place that no one else can understand. A frozen place. The way it feels to be blamed for someone else's death, when it was someone so close. It is enough to make anyone numb. Enough to make you shut down.

It is enough to make anyone want to push every thought, every creeping memory, far away from their mind, away from their heart.

*

Six months later. Over the hills and down. A secret like a bone hides like a pebble beneath the water. Its ripples are no longer visible on the surface. Other pebbles from the shore have clothed it, covered it, and forgotten it. But part of the secret, a whisper from cold, buried bones to heated flesh, still reaches out over the boggy landscape. The secret flies in the wind. A fragment of a death. It catches in the eyes of boy meets girl. The secret swirls in a pint glass, unseen, tasteless. It sparks between bodies and mouths that kiss.

*

It was Wednesday. The hump. Slap bang in the middle of the week. Somehow, the wrong day to get drunk. But Rachel didn't care about that.

Now she only thought about two things. Forgetting her grief in the pub every night looking for an antidote to loneliness, and wondering how she would get her body up for work the next morning.

She left the bookshop where she worked in Kendal, turned the key in the door and dropped the silver bundle into her bag. She stepped over the road, brushed her arm against the edge of the toyshop on the corner, and felt her body relax, but her bones sigh, as she entered the pub opposite.

She went up to the narrow bar. She could see the square opening of floor space where the toilets and the fruit machine were, where girls in short skirts and men in old jeans sang karaoke to an unmoved audience. Rachel drank at the bar on her own.

She watched as a woman took the microphone by the toilets and began to sing. Opposite, on the floor space, the woman's friend started dancing. Around her, the air and the ground where her feet moved were empty. A woman singing and her friend dancing, and everybody pretending they weren't paying them a grain of notice.

Beside Rachel someone coughed and ordered a pint. If she had been behind the bar she would have certainly thought about asking him for ID. The smell of the amber beer rose as the barmaid angled a glass against a pump. The lad paid his money over the bar, and drank in the creamy top of his pint. He turned to look at Rachel. She was watching the woman sing and the friend dance.

"If only they knew what they looked like, eh?" he said.

The music was loud, so she had to shout back to him, which she found ridiculous. Nearly didn't bother. "Well, at least they're having a good time," she answered.

"Oh?" he said. "So aren't you?"

Rachel looked at him. Sized him up. Not bad. Not brilliant, but not bad. He was young, anyway, that was one thing. That was different. She doubted she'd had one as young as this.

And no. Rachel wasn't having a good time.

She moved closer to him, smiled, and said, "Well, not yet, I'm not."

*

All her searching. Her scouring of people to find a warm place. Rachel Murdoch, unplanned daughter of an unplanned daughter, caught in the struggle of trapped women, couldn't know that men would all be cold too. No love here. Never any love.

It was dark and cold in the bedroom. Rachel had forgotten all about the heating when they came in. She'd stumbled through the door of her old terrace, didn't turn a light on or lock the door or anything. Her holding onto a scrunch of his coat, trying to keep her balance; him laughing at how drunk, how hopeless she was. Spilling into the house like beans.

She had, like she always had, the tiniest moment of regret as she lay down with this man. Mainly because she always thought about her gran and granddad and how they once occupied these rooms, how this had once been their house. Their bodies so blurred and melded together, their features a perfect mime of one another; sometimes it was hard to tell them apart. Fifty years of faithfulness blending them. They even became the same shade of grey. And here was Rachel, their only grandchild, throwing away their memories, and her own mind, giving away her body. Again and again. Her grandparents would be turning if either of them had a grave. She knew it. She was beginning to feel it drag on her, the feeling old and pointless. So many men.

They weren't all young, but this one, who hadn't bought Rachel a single drink tonight in the pub (why did she decide to bring this one home?) was the youngest so far. She'd wondered if that would make a difference. She'd hoped his innocence, his unbroken heart, his unshaped cynicism would mean something.

It hadn't.

He still did the same things, moved in the same way. Their limbs a tangle of slippery bone, cold and impatient. Showed her no tenderness. It was warm for a brief moment. Between them. Then he told her a story, his arm holding her limply as if they'd been thrown together and he had no choice.

It was a story that had spark, that scared her; woke her. It was about a woman who had a dream that she was going to be attacked by the bloke she was with.

"Are you making this up?" Rachel asked.

He shrugged. But she could see his smile in the darkness, his big mouth, his teeth shining.

Rachel drew her body away from him slightly and tried to look into his eyes. She didn't like the way he was talking. Realised, stupidly, that he could be anyone, could do anything.

"But she killed him first and dumped his body in a lake. Buttermere."

Buttermere. On that first night Rachel had gone to the pub after work, the girls from the other shops had been talking about what had happened in Buttermere. That day when it was the last thing in the world she wanted to talk about.

"You think that's all right though, don't you?" he said. "Because she thought he was going to kill her."

"Depends," she said.

"On...?"

"On whether the bloke really was going to kill her. It's never *right*, is it?" she said. "But I suppose circumstances—"

"Exactly. Circumstances. And maybe she killed him by accident and then she just didn't know what to do."

"Oh yeah," said Rachel. Wishing he would shut up now.

"But he didn't *know* he was going to."

"What?"

"The bloke who was killed. He didn't know he was going to kill her. "

Rachel was relieved by a tiny slip in his tone, putting the story back out into the past, and she didn't answer. She pushed herself down in the bed again, under the duvet that was sealed in a cover she'd had God knows how long, that she'd washed and hung on the line so many times the material had rubbed itself into tiny bobbles as if it was trying to escape bit by bit. She slid like a knot on a wire, back between the boy's arm and his chest. She liked this place best of all. When she got to lay herself alongside someone.

In the darkness Rachel could feel his breath.

"I bet she wasn't sorry though," he muttered.

14

Why did he have to bring that girl up again?

His flesh was sighing next to her. But Rachel couldn't sleep. Why had he told her that story? She was still awake when he woke quickly and made a stupid remark about his mother being worried, which Rachel sneered at. He wasn't *that* young.

And then he left. He hadn't even stayed for twenty minutes after. Pulled on his trousers in the darkness, fastened his shirt and carried his coat over his arm. But Rachel was relieved he was going, and taking his stories with him.

She listened as he ran down the old, steep staircase, the tatty worn carpet dirt grey under his shoes, then out the front door, the slam of the wood making the chain and the letterbox chime together. She remembered his face for a short while as she lay in her bed, staring at the sky through open curtains. But by the time she got up the next morning, it was all but gone.

Rachel had tiny, bulbous tears in her eyes when she ran for the bus that morning. No idea why. Why should she care if the boy didn't even stay? She was actually glad when he had gone.

She knew he wouldn't come back, they never did, and she didn't want him to, but they usually at least stay till the morning creeps over the sky. Then they leave. They always leave. Everybody, she thought, always leaves.

She stuck her arm out like a cyclist turning a corner as she slowed down to meet the bus. Felt exposed doing it. She could feel the skin of her face burn like a deep dream while she handed her money to the driver. Spoke her destination. And watched him as he ignored everything about her.

Was she even there?

On the bus to Kendal, alone, nothing had ever felt so cold. She watched the diving roads turn, wind throwing itself recklessly into the trees. And surprised herself by thinking about her mother, even more so, her father. Far away from her now.

"Well," Rachel's mum had said before they went, "You'll still be able to visit, it's not as if we'll be on the other side of the world."

Disconnected from their responsibilities. Having a life somewhere. Trying to have the life they'd never been able to have here. Forgetting Rachel and everything else they'd left behind.

Rachel wished, sometimes, pathetically, that she could do the same. Just forget it. This stupid place. This hole. Forget everything and start again. Maybe somewhere new. Or maybe just with someone. But she never did. Couldn't. This was her home, this lame village. She hadn't left when she had the chance and now *things* seemed to tie her here. Like guy ropes. People and her memories of them covering her like polythene.

Rachel couldn't remember the face of the boy from last night at all now. She was trying, but it had become a shape moving under water. As for his name, she was no longer sure if she'd ever known that in the first place. She sighed into the glass of the bus window. She was getting too old for this.

Kendal greeted Rachel as it does every morning, as if welcoming her with open arms. Rachel got off the bus and stood with her hand rummaging in her bag for a moment. She felt like it was the end of something. The end of so many men. Can't do this any more. And anyway, this one scared her. Who knows what a man might be capable of? She felt a rush all over her body as the slots of reality connected. What had she been expecting to find? It was always the same. Every man was the same. They couldn't give her back what was missing.

She pulled a small packet of contraceptive pills from a zipped flap in her bag. Looked at them for a moment. Her backup. An innocent little tray of white pills that tricked her body over and over again. And her womb never got the joke, never realised.

She stuffed them into the bin by the bus stop and walked away, on to the book shop where she worked. Onto Finkle Street.

16

*

And now five more years have gone by. The water still covers the bone. But the currents unsettle it in its resting place. Suppressing it so its deformities feel even more mis-shapen every day. It wants to rise to the surface. It needs to come out into the open to join with the chipped and sharp fragment of itself which is still out there somewhere. Only then can the dark secret heal itself.

*

Sunday night. The narrow path at the roadside felt dangerous. Like a mountain pass instead of a pavement. The wheels of cars were skimming front doors and spraying rain from puddles onto the windows.

Rachel walked away from her small house, carrying a gift protectively in her arms, holding it as if she might rock it to sleep. A thick encyclopaedia, bursting with photographs and descriptions of plants and flowers, trees and fruits, which Will probably didn't need, she realised. He probably understood everything there was to understand about this stuff already. But Rachel didn't know him well enough to think of anything else to give him. She only had this one snip of information that linked her to him. And it had been short notice.

She picked the book from the shelf at work the day before, wrapped it carefully in thick paper she bought at the newsagent in the village. Didn't get him a card. Cards are so difficult to choose for people, she thought, especially people you hardly know.

She shifted the heavy book in her arms as she stopped at the traffic lights. The green man appeared, then flickered while the cars revved, and Rachel walked over to the pub on the corner.

It made a change to be asked out these days. Not a date of course, nothing like that, Rachel didn't do dates. Everybody, even Will, she presumed, knew that. For a moment, she wondered what he knew about her. Had he heard how she used to behave, how she used to treat flesh like food?

But it never worked. In the end, she realised, sleeping around could never have filled her up. And anyway, you want to *savour* something, not have the experience pass you by before you could even taste it. Rachel still wanted to savour, and even to taste something new for the first time.

It was strange how she had met Will. How an invisible, intricate language grew between them. As if the tiny movement of their fingers on flowers was a whisper. A code.

They began to talk in the garden centre at Grasmere only last week. Rachel buying small, pretty pot plants, delicate like kittens, that she could carry on her lap on the bus back to their village. He running his hands over the giant egg-shaped water fountains and sketching gardens in his mind that would involve elaborate patio designs, rubbing wine red leaves between his fingers, saying words like 'Forsythia' and 'Kalanchoe' to himself. Sounding out the Latin name for each plant as if constructing a running list on his tongue of all the things he would buy.

He was a strange one, she realised. Rachel could see it instantly.

He shifted amongst the tall trees and the sprawling shrubs as if he was one of them. As if they alone understood him.

Rachel watched him for a while. Ashamed to admit, she followed him. Around the Japanese Maples, by a wall of trellis, under a patio heater like a street lamp. When he turned and noticed her, she tested him. Gave him the eye. Couldn't help it. Just couldn't stop herself.

What was wrong with her? But he had smiled and, eventually, mumbling something about the two empty seats by the door, sat down with her in the café. He told her about his work with the private firm of landscapers, about how terrible the money was.

"I left school..." Will stopped and seemed to be struggling to continue. "Well, I didn't get my exams, so... maybe if I'd tried harder at school I could have got a better job."

Then he shrugged. "It's all right," he said, and Rachel got the feeling he was sparing her the discomfort of being faced with his failings.

She waited for him to tell her his dreams and ambitions, to

siphon from his heart an acceptable, tell-able version of deep and old longings. But he just stared at the sugar he was dumping in swirls on the table like a finger trail in sand. And Rachel felt the pull of her age. That the prickly memory of school still chased Will so closely.

"Me neither," she said. "Of course, it's a little longer since I was at school…" She felt him look up from the table then. Let the point sink into his eyes. "But that isn't everything, is it?" she said.

She realised there was a double meaning to what she had said, and in that instant assented deep down within herself that their age difference did not have to get in her way. But she needed to clarify herself. "Exams and that, I mean – there's more to life."

She wanted to keep the conversation going all afternoon, even though Will didn't seem the type to *chat*. She found out that he grew up in Manchester and that he'd grown plants for as long as he could remember. But he didn't tell her much else.

So she talked about her garden at home where she grew plump courgettes, runner beans and five different types of tomato. Couldn't stop growing things, she said. It was what came of being brought up by grandparents in a backwater village. She pushed it. Talked it up. No TV. Nothing else to do. Never mentioned her parents. And she felt the semi-truths like her old endless come-ons to unsuitable men waking him up.

Her reward came when she told him where she lived. Will smiled so hard it not only opened up his face but it looked like he would break.

"I can't believe it," he said. "Me too."

Rachel was just as pleased, even if she was cool enough not to show it.

"I mean not down in the village like you," Will continued, "but up on that new estate, do you know it? Hilltop."

"Yeah. Yeah, I know it." she said, desperate to keep the words flowing. Keep him talking like this with the smile that creased the tired skin below his eyes. "God, the locals hate you lot," she said. "Buying new houses on what used to be a scenic old hill, set of bloody thieves, you are!"

"What?"

Rachel laughed. "You know how those old farts down in the village think. You lot have come in and taken land that they used to stare at from their kitchen windows and turned it into a miniature suburb. They hate that. They'll never forgive you."

She could see that he didn't know how to take it. The strand of engagement between them was too thin for him to understand that she was teasing him.

She thought for a minute that she'd blown it.

Painfully, she wondered if he would care. He stared at her, the smile still, until she said, "I'm only joking." And then he laughed.

Rachel knew then that *she* would have cared. She felt the familiar sink of early, reckless attachment, in her ribcage. Checked it. Felt older for it. Thought, she couldn't let this happen. She knew it was a feeling that always impaled itself in a rejection.

It was suicide to let herself slip into this. She'd promised herself she'd never do it again. She had grown used to expecting nothing more than dead ends in everything: her search for meaning with random men had trained her to believe love was a lie told to children. So being single was just another part of life that she would have to bear, alongside a job with no prospects, the gap left by her parents, and a phone book empty of true friends.

And then, with his dirty, stubby fingers crushing the sugar on the table, Will asked her if she was busy on Sunday.

It was nothing, he said, with a swift shrug of his shoulder. It didn't matter. Just a stupid party his mother had arranged, and he had to be there. But he would like her to be there too.

Rachel had a new feeling, new to her, of being chosen.

The old inn was wrapped around the end of the street down in the bottom of the village. A sticking plaster covering the gap between the stone houses and little shops that led away from it in both directions. The front of the building had once been painted red but now its skin has faded to a dulled pink. Rachel looked at it as she crossed the road. It was the same as the other buildings really, she thought. Just like people are all the same underneath. She shouldn't expect too much of anyone, shouldn't expect too much of Will. She'd only end up being disappointed. It was only stone, she told herself. Just like people are only flesh. All the same. If you scratch the surface, people bleed. Like everything else, if you scratch away at the paint, underneath is just like all the rest.

It was William's 21st birthday party. In the pub on the corner at the crossroads in the village, where lorries scream through the traffic lights and all the way on up to Scotland, their bulky frames shuddering into the cold north. Rachel thought she felt a shiver herself when she pushed the door at eight o'clock that night. Some kind of foretelling in her flesh which the 21st century had taught her to ignore. She entered the pub, hitching the heavy book onto her hip again. The smell of old, damp, smoke-saturated furniture fell into her face. There was a roar like the noise she would hear coming up from under water.

She blushed and looked around her. But the roar died as soon as it was born. It was nothing. Nothing to do with her. No one was looking at her: not the ladies' darts team playing in the corner, nor the group of men in cotton shirts and jeans, all holding bottles of French lager, standing in a tattered semi-circle near the bar.

It was a party, that was all, Rachel told herself. She just happened to walk in at that moment when the butt of a joke was kicked into life or the call for more beer was thrown over the bar.

She stood for a second by the door, picking off the people like ticks on a page until her eyes came to Will.

Will was seated. He was wearing black canvas trousers, shoes not trainers, and a blue shirt with three stripes running through it like dreams. His hair appeared darker than she remembered: in the garden centre she had been close enough to see the redness bleed through. It had been cut earlier today. She immediately noticed his fringe, curtailed like chopped daffodil stalks, and as she approached she could see the tiny flecks at the back of his neck that had been resistant to the barber's brush.

Rachel edged her way in, and she gave Will the book, brushed his cheek with the corner of her mouth, smelled the warmed aftershave at his jaw-line. He had bones in his cheeks like ice in cloth, like teeth in a kiss.

What did she feel, there, in that moment? She'd kid herself their souls met. She told herself over and over, though she knew it wasn't true, that the essence of who they were, hundreds of years old, knew one another, recognised instantly their fate. Just how it must have been when her gran first met her granddad.

Then she moved away as more guests arrived with handshakes and jokes about him being a man now. She stood by one of the tables and smiled as a middle-aged man brought drinks back from the bar.

"Hello love," he said. "You a friend of Will's then?"

"Sort of," she replied.

The man held out his hand to shake hers. "I'm Will's boss," he said.

She put her hand in his. "Rachel."

He was a little red in the face and looked as if he'd had a couple too many drinks already. He sat down at the table and took a big gulp from his pint, as another man sat down at the table with him.

She saw the knowing look in their eyes and immediately felt

herself becoming the object of rumour and speculation. Turned away. Looked around for a moment. Then tried to make polite conversation with one of Will's cousins. He told her he had come from Manchester for the weekend specially.

"So did you spend a lot of time with Will when he lived in Manchester?" Rachel asked.

The cousin looked blank.

"You know, when you were kids together. You must be about the same age as him."

"But Will didn't live in Manchester," he said, confused. "Before they came here they lived in—"

But he stopped himself sharply, and looked at Rachel suspiciously.

"How did you say you know him?" he asked.

"Oh, we're just… friends," she said, tailing off lamely as Will's cousin shifted his gaze to look over her shoulder, not really interested in the answer, and made an excuse to go over to another part of the pub.

Rachel stood alone for a while, just watching the comings and goings, wondering how long she would have to wait for someone to come up and talk to her. She looked across at the bar. Will was… let's face it, Rachel thought, as she watched him; he didn't like being the centre of attention. He looked uncomfortable. Dying inside. He needed rescuing just as much as she did. Everyone was battering him with questions. *How's it feel lad? Key to the door and all that.*

"Hey Will," one of them shouted, "Jenny behind the bar's getting the tequila out. Come on mate, you're in there!"

Everybody laughed. And he hated it. He dipped his head to hide his eyes, shoved his hands in his pockets and shrugged his shoulders. And all Rachel wanted to do was to pluck him out. He didn't belong here. He was different.

She caught Will's eye... again. It felt like the abrupt *tock* of two cogs, ceasing to move on once they'd fallen into place.

Was it happening again? Five years of nothing but her own body had made her desperate, she thought. But he was still looking at her. And she could feel it, just happening. His stare. Her body. Was there any other way to do this?

She took a couple of steps forward.

There are things that pass between people that no one else can see.

There was an argument starting up by the fruit machine. And Will's cousin was calling Will back to the bar, holding out a tall glass filled with ice, a straw and God knows what else. But Will ignored them all, consumed in one moment, moving silently towards Rachel.

Who would have thought so much could be said in that way?

*

Will and Rachel left the pub holding hands. She felt for him in the semi-darkness; red, amber, green of the traffic lights beside them, and there was no danger of her being rejected now. She told herself that it would be different this time.

They crossed the road, running while cars turned right into the village square, and began walking up the hill. Rachel slowed as they passed level with her windows, wondering if Will knew which house she lived in. When she looked at him he was gazing across with her.

They could see each headlight from the passing cars held for a second in the little transparent discs of a wind-chime at her window, and then a stream of white, like a strobe, dash over the Mexican rug on the far wall.

She'd nailed that up as noisily as possible when her

neighbours, fresh from their forced grief over the death of Rachel's gran, had told her she needed to keep the net curtains, to stop potential burglars from peering in. She had been so angry with them for daring to interfere, for pretending they cared about her, that she had been looking forward to telling them the shape on the rug was a red and black snake eagle that would give the would-be burglars something to look at. It did seem a ridiculous sight now, and she felt the need to explain it somehow, blurting out, "My grandparents are dead. That's who I lived with, my gran and granddad, but they're dead now."

As soon as she said it she realised that she never talked about this. Not really. Had never had anyone to talk to about it. She'd told the necessary people when first her granddad died and later her gran. She'd told her boss at the bookshop so he understood why she wasn't at work. Told her neighbours because she had to. And she told her mum and dad by letter. Couldn't even face doing that on the phone, didn't want to hear their voices, to answer their questions. But apart from that Rachel had never talked about this.

The realisation filled her belly with a strange mix of chemicals. Stale grief. Disappointment. Relief.

Will didn't ask her about it. He didn't ask where her parents were or if they were dead too. Didn't allow her any pity. He was trailing his fingers over the leaves of an overhanging bush, almost speaking to the thing with his touch.

He ignored what she'd said and pointed at gardens as they passed them on their way up the hill, saying, "I did that one. Look, see that palm tree over there, I planted that."

Rachel could follow the pride on his face when he talked about his work, from his eyes, down each side of his face, around his mouth. Then he would close down his own happiness, shrugging and saying, "Of course, most of the time I only do bloody patios. Most of the time it's shit." And Rachel thought she could talk to him about anything, talk forever, and he'd never judge.

They reached the top of the hill and Will opened the door to his house quickly. He said it was cold out there. Made that into a reason to get inside.

She looked at him as he twisted his key in the lock. In the light from neighbouring houses his finely freckled skin appeared pinpricked with sand. Earthy. Timeless. Will opened the door. They stepped inside the small house. And he locked it again behind them.

Inside the house the ceilings were low. The kitchen was a fifth of the size of Rachel's and the stairway led *down* to the bedrooms instead of up. There was something wrong with this house. She could feel it just like she could feel rain in the air before it began to fall from the clouds. Someone who understood *Feng Shui* could probably tell her what it was. There was something about the atmosphere in the house that was just... what exactly? Off balance somehow.

Rachel wanted to look around. She'd never been in one of these new houses before. But Will held onto her hands. He leaned forward and kissed her by the spindle banister that led down the stairs.

Rachel could feel his warm skin through his shirt as she put her arms around him. She could smell the scent he sprayed near his jaw line when he'd got dressed tonight and beneath that, the bare scent of his skin.

She finished the kiss, but she continued to look into his eyes. She already knew she was falling too quickly. Before he led her to the staircase Rachel saw on the wall beside them the red light on the answering machine pulsing like a warning.

Downstairs in Will's room, where the back door opened onto the garden and again, into the hill, Rachel undressed quickly and straddled him before he'd even finished unbuttoning his shirt. The night lights of cars swooped over the walls of his bedroom. She helped him loosen his belt and unzipped his trousers, laughing while he struggled with the last two buttons caught in the holes on his shirt.

She began, almost forgetting.

"Wait!" Will reached into the drawer beside the bed. "Wait," he said. "We should... unless you are...? Are you?"

She shook her head and pulled her leg away, kneeling on the single bed. "No," she said. "I'm not on the pill if that's what you mean, and yeah, we should anyway."

She waited for Will, and when he was ready she began again. Still taking the lead. She sensed the way he was making his moves very apprehensively and she wondered for a moment whether he'd ever tried to impress any of the girls he'd taken to bed before.

Then he rolled over, becoming more confident, but still clumsily taking her with him, then under him like a curled wave.

Rachel knew as soon as it happened. She felt it. But Will didn't seem to realise at all. Only when he had finished, and knelt back on the bed, he cursed, "Shit, look at that."

He picked at the condom with his fingers like tweezers. "It's split, that's so crap." He threw it to one side, broken and useless. Rachel could see the worry beginning as he lay back down beside her and closed his eyes.

*

In a chapel, freezing cold.

Will's mum had made them all wear layers that day. Vest. T-shirt. Jumper. Waterproof coat. But even with two pairs of socks his mum could do nothing about the numbness shutting down Will's toes. Bit by bit, edging further up his feet. If this carried on, he'd lose all sensation up to his knees.

He'd been outside. Went past a pub. Too young to go in. But asking himself now, why hadn't he tried it? Could have asked for a coke or something. Bet they had a real fire in there. Bet there were plenty of people all taking their coats off and talking and laughing, drinking and oozing warmth. He thought about going back out.

The others. He needed to let the others know where he was. But his feet simply wouldn't co-operate. He was too cold. So he sat in the pews, staring at the walls. And hugged his body.

*

Will was lying in the darkness. Awake again. Had been dreaming something. But he was letting it slip away from him again already.

He let it go; let it slide back under water. If he wanted to catch it, he thought, maybe he could dredge everything out with a net and then find it... whatever it was.

But Will doesn't fish. And it stayed in the water. It was easier that way.

A car rolled down the hill beside his window. He could hear voices outside the house. His dad. His mum. Saying goodnight to the neighbours. He looked at the clock cradled on a chair in the corner and saw through the dim and dusty air that it was after midnight. He tried to move his arm, but it felt numb. Then he remembered something.

It was Rachel, asleep beside him. He turned. Took breath in. He'd been with Rachel. It seemed like a trick for a moment, like she'd wake and laugh at how easily he'd been fooled or else disappear and become the dream he believed her to be.

He pulled his arm from under her shoulders and tried to sit up as her breath threatened to stir. He looked down at her and still found it vaguely astonishing that she was there. In the darkness he could see that Rachel's skin was almost as pale as his own. White like a dull moon. Her hair, that had previously been pulled to the back of her head by a scarf, was like reels of film from an old camera all over her face, the pillow, her bare arms. Tea-coloured. Coiled. Like bruised apple peel held on a knife blade. He wanted to touch it. Stupid. He'd already touched much more than that. But for some reason the thing they'd just done, sex, seemed less intimate.

He could hear his dad's key in the door upstairs and he had to wake Rachel somehow. He knew his mum would come in and wish him good night, happy birthday again. And he knew she couldn't see this woman lying asleep in his bed. He gently rocked Rachel's shoulders.

"Rachel! Rachel, wake up!" he whispered.

She pushed his hand away, mid-regaining consciousness. Then opened her eyes. She didn't look at all surprised to see him. He wondered how he'd managed to push it from his mind while he dozed beside her and yet she'd kept it right there. She smiled. And Will said, "Rachel, my mum and dad are here, you'll have to hide."

"What? Are you joking?" She giggled then, and he could almost believe she was one of the girls he had been to school with, the same age as him, younger even. He stared at her in the darkness and shook his head.

"Just for a moment. Just while my mum comes in."

"But where?"

He looked around him at the cold, empty bedroom. The single wardrobe packed with his work clothes and boots. The tall chest of drawers by the back door. He pulled open the covers and grabbed her arm. "Just lie on the floor down here. And be quiet."

She'd stopped smiling now and she looked at him with a

mixture of disbelief and disgust. But she got on the floor and lay down next to the wall anyway, where the wool carpet was itchy against the skin on her back and legs. He seemed so frantic to hide her.

Will had arranged the sheets over his body neatly by the time the door opened and his mum stood there. "What happened to you?" she demanded. "It was supposed to be your party, you could have stayed."

He struggled in the bright slice of light for words. "I was tired," he said. "Anyway, parties aren't my thing."

"God, listen to you, *parties aren't my thing*. You should be grateful."

Will stared at the duvet covering his body. He could hear Rachel's breath against the wall. His face turned and pleaded with his mum to leave him alone.

"You know I don't really like—"

"Don't really like much of anything, William, do you?" his mum said. "You should try and be more like your brother. He's still down there now, persuading the landlord to carry on serving." She started to close the door. Seemed to sniff something in the air. Shook her head. "Happy birthday," she said, and closed the door.

The room was dark again. It was quiet. They could hear the kettle begin to breathe in the kitchen upstairs and the mugs knock awkwardly as Will's mum got them from the cupboard. Rachel stayed down on the floor between the single bed and the wall. Wondered for a moment what she was doing there, hiding from this boy's mother. It was ridiculous at Rachel's age. She wanted to tell Will to stop acting like such a kid and stand up to his mum, stand up for Rachel and stop acting like he was ashamed of what they'd done. But he was young, she reminded herself. A lot younger than Rachel. Maybe she shouldn't expect him to behave any other way.

After a while she heard Will say, "It's OK, you can get up now."

"We'll wait a bit longer," he said. "Then I'll pretend I'm going to the loo and I'll let you out."

They both got dressed. He didn't touch her again, but he held her hand as he fumbled with his key in the darkness, unlocking the French doors that led out onto the garden from his bedroom. The doors relaxed and he dashed out into the hall to flush the toilet and then hurry back while the noise of the water rushed round the house. Rachel stepped outside onto the garden. He kissed her once, goodbye kiss, then quickly locked the door and went back to bed.

Will's mum, Cath, got up in the middle of the night. Her bladder had never been the same since she'd borne her children and spent hours with other mothers downing ever-flowing cups of tea. She ran her hand lightly over her stomach and thought about how it used to feel, years ago, and she wondered why nature has to be so cruel. She was once a slim girl, a woman with an impressive body, and a smile. She used to have internal organs that did their jobs properly and didn't dictate terms to her brain in the middle of the night. Whereas now, if nothing else wakes her – her husband snoring or the rain pelting the windows – the heavy ball of pressure on her bladder surely will.

She opened her bedroom door and paused on the landing. Yellow light was bleeding under Will's door and onto the carpet in front of her feet like a sudden spill of water.

Cath experienced an unusual moment of uncertainty before she went into the bathroom.

Had Will's birthday party unlocked some emotion? Was it something someone had said to him? Had someone said something they shouldn't have?

They were all drinking a lot in the pub, especially Martin, and maybe one of the other kids had let some words ooze from his mouth. Or one of her own friends, loosened by whisky and forgetting for a second that they just don't talk about it.

That would explain why he had left so early.

Cath didn't see Will leave the party. She had only noticed later that he was no longer there.

But she knew she'd been hiding her eyes away from him in the crowds. Still couldn't look at him sometimes, especially at parties: at any other kind of celebration. It wasn't right.

Was he awake because a curl of his memories had been shoved...? She almost went in to see him. Pictured him, with a face full of bewilderment and tears, and suddenly willing to talk.

But then she realised she was being stupid. She knew it. He would have fallen asleep reading or watching TV without switching the light off. Will was always doing that. Always watching pointless TV by himself and reading those stupid things, what did he call them? Graphic novels? Comics more like. Always alone, that was Will. And it was nothing more than he deserved.

Cath wondered for a single, rooted moment, if perhaps she was too hard on him. The thought flew away almost as quickly as it had come to her. He was all right. He was always all right. That was the problem. Things always turned out all right for Will. It wasn't fair.

She felt the sickening plunge of it in her stomach then. Why didn't she know him? She'd given birth to him, grown him in her body. How could he be so cold?

Every time she looked at him she couldn't ignore all the lies and the denial. And she didn't mind admitting that she hated him.

This wasn't the way it was supposed to be. Cath wished daily that Will could be more like Martin. Wished hourly that she'd never bothered in the first place. But it was all too late.

She went into the bathroom and switched on the light.

When she came out the light in Will's bedroom had gone off at last. He made sure of it, not wanting to be disturbed, and pulled the covers up to his neck. Smelled an unfamiliar warm fuzz on the sheets. Breathed it in. Hoped it could cancel out the uneasiness that had woken him before. And when he did sleep, Rachel's hair curled between his fingers in his dream.

*

The rain is sliding down the road. An oil-slick ooze. Into puddles, bursting them like a runny egg yolk.

Rachel clings to a window and watches for any sign, any cosmic reassurance.

Every second since last night seems to be empty, and at the same time full, of every tiny detail about him. She wants to know everything. She wants to know everything there is to know about him right now. It can't wait.

It feels like she must capture his whole life inside her now, or it could be lost. Exactly the way it must have been when her gran had first met her granddad. The same emotions sliding down the years, she's sure.

She fingers the edge of a slat in the wooden blind at the window, and realises she must have been standing there staring at the way the ends of each piece of wood have warped in the sun for at least twenty minutes. And the time has passed like the swoop of a single gull. Is that what's been missing all these years? Someone whose presence in her mind made every tiny detail in life seem huge?

She paces her kitchen. Knows she should tidy up the mess, wash some pots, free the hall carpet from the flecks of sawdust left there by the guinea pigs. Rachel often brings her guinea pigs into the house, petting them on her knee and un-matting their fur with a soft, doll-like brush. They leave trails of shredded paper from their hutches, and wisps of fur from the brush, all over the floor.

She should tidy up, she knows, but her mind won't let her settle.

He is a thought she can't capture. An image she's seen only once and just can't replicate.

Must hold back. Don't give it away too quickly, too easily.

She moves in the silent kitchen. Feels the sway of time in her long skirt, the death of her grandparents still a black place in her life. And then the light coming through. She hears her gran in her head. Can almost touch the words as they circle her. And she wonders if Will is experiencing identical thoughts and emotions to those of Rachel's granddad, Arthur Barnes, all those years before.

*

Tireless thieving formed the backbone of the Barnes family. In the same way that some families are held together by love, or duty, or circumstance, and some by debt, the Barnes family were held firmly in place by Arthur's father, Mr. Barnes, and his sticky fingers. He was a great tree of a man. Huge. With shoulders like a Queen Anne bed frame. A thick torso that planted itself in a room and would not be moved till it had done with the air. Mr. Barnes commanded respect. Demanded it. Would use his fists and the bulk of his body to gain it. Got whatever he wanted. He led two of his sons into an identical life of corrosive crime, digging deeper into the blackness of the unsuspecting people on the streets of Leeds.

Even his youngest son, who was not his own, became an expert in the fine art of thuggery once Mr Barnes finally decided to make an asset of him. Despite the more tender strands of another man's DNA coiled in his body, he happily followed the Barnes line and fought for his place in the city, demanding all the respect and reward his meaty fists could bring him.

But not the second youngest son. Not Arthur. The last to be born before Mr. Barnes' one and only stint in a cold prison cell, the genuine end of the Barnes line, the runt of a fearsome litter. Only Arthur refused. Only Arthur, with his small body and his gentle manner, ignored his father. He would rather go walking, rescue a stray cat, or scrub the front steps of the house, than follow his father anywhere. Even when Mr. Barnes happily slapped Arthur's mother in front of him and asked if she hadn't made some mistake and maybe this little bastard wasn't his either, Arthur still sat mutely, emotionless and still refused to go anywhere with his father.

Inevitably Arthur was thrown out. His mother pleaded with Mr. Barnes for a full ten minutes, sitting at the kitchen table, with a milk bottle and half a loaf unmoved on the table, until she gave up, shrugged her shoulders, turned her head and wafted Arthur away with her hand.

With a single bag Arthur travelled west, towards the sea. He had an idea that he'd trace the maternal line of his family all the way back over the water to Ireland, but instead he followed the lure of the mountains and the lakes, where the fields were like low breaths blown over the earth, and he settled on the southern tip of Cumbria.

Mary was fifteen when Arthur first spotted her. Aged eighteen, Arthur had found himself a job digging deep under the earth in the black mines. After work he drank beer as black as the coal he sliced from the tunnel walls with the other men. They would walk straight to the pub, their faces smeared and dusted with deathly powder. And on Saturdays they scrubbed their bodies raw until the blood prickled beneath their skin, in order to jostle their way into the local cinema.

Every week in that dark little theatre Arthur saw Mary. Every week he had no idea what to say to her. She made the air struggle in his chest, his words back up in his throat. The only way he could do it was with beer inside him.

The night Arthur leapt over all the seats in the cinema to land on the empty one beside her, Mary didn't seem to notice that his breath was fogged with beer and his eyes were swimming in their sockets. Nor did she seem to mind that his hands wandered a little too much when he kissed her. Arthur was a mystery. He wasn't local. He came by himself at the age of eighteen and wouldn't speak about his past at all. He was the one all the girls wanted to know about. He was unusual. Complicated perhaps. He was different, and Mary definitely liked that.

He was like a dream. Sent from some magical place. He was made of heart-stopping love, his bones wrapped in faultless skin.

When the opportunity came for Arthur to try and take things further, Mary didn't say no to him. How could she? It was only a few weeks after she'd first met him, but she knew he was the one for her and she couldn't refuse him anything. They waited one Saturday and sneaked into his lodgings when the rest of the household was out.

Upstairs, as he moved on top of her, Mary felt each brush of Arthur's body against hers like a spark of fire in cold leaves. He was making assurances to her. It would be OK, he said. She should trust him. But it hurt like hell. Mary wanted to push him off at first, this couldn't be normal. But her infatuation with him seemed to overpower all the pain and discomfort, all the panic.

In the end, Mary concentrated on Arthur's fingers that were tensing by her head. He had the most beautiful fingers. She could see the black in his nails, the cuts striking out the natural lines, the rough palm of his hand and the split knuckles. They were not pretty, but when Arthur touched Mary, his fingers felt like tiny feathers. Her skin puckered to it and she was lost. She could put up with the pain, the impossibility of what he was doing. She could put up with anything. This was definitely love.

Nine months later and love had been taken over. Passed like mist over a moon by the massive presence of a baby. Mary touched her stomach and felt her shame kick and burn. She'd dreamed all her life of the wedding she would have. Her mother had planned for it, along with the weddings of Mary's sisters. Her father had put something by for it. And Mary herself had arranged bouquets of perfection in her mind and had always meant to keep her dignity for it. Now she would hush through the day, her dress altered beyond recognition to allow for the swell of her shame, her face barely allowed a smile. And then she would absorb into her life the body she had brought about. She would be a wife, a mother. She would follow the tracks. While Arthur did his work and drank his beer and spent every other shred of time turning over earth in his stupid, beloved allotment, Mary would slowly die. And she seriously doubted if anybody would even notice.

There are no photos of Rachel's grandparents' wedding. The *plus one* hiding in the bride's stomach rendered that impossible. But Rachel didn't mind. It made them seem more human. Everyone makes mistakes.

She stands and looks past the rain and into the back garden. Doesn't want to think about how many mistakes she's made. Doesn't want to make any more. She wonders if she has it right this time. How can anyone be sure? She doesn't know everything about Will. But then Rachel's gran can't have known everything about her granddad when they were first together. Especially because Rachel knows her granddad had a mysterious past, a life before The Lakes. But it turned out all right for them, didn't it?

The uncomfortably conceived baby, Andrea, Rachel's mother, grew. Out-grew everything and everybody. At school she passed friends over the minute she was bored with them. As a teenager she slammed the front door in the faces of boys when she'd done with them. She never took care of her parents in their old age. She

39

passed that job swiftly onto her own daughter, Rachel. And Andrea was always amazed, and relieved, by how willingly Rachel did it.

Arthur died first, leaving Rachel the legacy of his allotment which she had taken over both dutifully and eagerly. Mary, who'd been dying for so long, lived on. Until one winter a few years later while Rachel was away and her gran didn't bother with the heating. Had had enough. Died of hypothermia in her old armchair by her unlit fire. Everybody said she was still pining for Arthur, even after all these years. Couldn't live without him, and she just gave up on the useless struggle of life and died. But, of course, the truth was much blander than that.

Rachel knew her gran wouldn't have died of a broken heart after so many years of living without Arthur, but she knew she was tired of life. And it wasn't that much of a surprise when she was found dead in her armchair.

The surprise was that when Rachel arrived home from a week's training course the door had been broken down and the police were waiting for her. Rachel's neighbours hadn't seen Mary for days and had called 999, accusing Rachel of neglecting her.

Rachel was even more upset about being blamed for it. Surely the neighbours knew she had always been close to her gran? Of course she had phoned her while she was away that week – and Mary seemed fine.

Rachel did know her gran was giving up on life. She'd felt it for weeks. But Rachel still couldn't believe it when it happened. At least the police didn't bother her for long: they could see how upset she was, and dismissed the neighbours' unnecessary accusations. But when Mary's body had been taken away, Rachel sat back on the floor and cried. She felt the silence in the house close in on her. She was really alone now.

She was the only one there to use the things that had once

belonged to her gran. Saucepans. The teapot. An old glass mixing bowl. The only person left to handle her gran's jewellery and sort through piles of photos and letters.

There was no one else to pass the house to either, just like the allotment tucked behind the village. So it passed on to Rachel. By then it was her home, after all.

*

Later, the windows streaked with salt and the guttering still dripping, Rachel steps from the back door, down the three stone steps. Dead heads the hanging baskets on her way, tossing the brown petals onto the grass. She picks up a large tub of fish food and idly sprinkles some into the pond. Then she sits on the damp steps and leans over the Perspex sheet she's propped up against the wall.

She watches the guinea pigs wriggling around inside the hutch, their curled backs balls of fur as they sleep or snuggle against each other.

What had happened last night? She's still trying to work it out. Rachel had had flings before, a long time ago, mainly one night stands with men from the pub in Kendal who she met after work.

This was different. She could still sense him on her body. Still feel him. His smell had laid itself on her skin and wouldn't budge. This was it. Just like she'd stepped into her dreams. And there was no going back now. He could cut into her and fill all the gaps in her body. He could fill the hole her family had left.

*

She travelled to work on the bus that Monday as she did every morning, but this time it felt totally different. No, that was wrong.

41

It had never felt of anything before. Today the seat on the bus where she sat down had a strange effect on her legs. The cold hand rail startled her palms. The button, when she pressed it for her stop, seemed to be reacting to the pressure from her thumb in a way she was sure it reacted to no one else.

Everything was different.

She walked the streets. Smelled the doughnuts, even at this hour, from the bakery. Heard the cups clink in the café on Finkle Street. Flinched as she caught sight of the pub.

Inside the bookshop in Kendal Rachel took off her coat. Shook it slightly like a wet dog in drizzle. Hung it up in the little room at the back of the shop. She muttered *morning* at her boss who didn't move his eyes or his attention away from the magazine he had flat on the counter. And she felt the feeling of amazement at every individual thing begin to flake away from her.

Rachel flicked the switch on the kettle and lifted her mug from the circular tray on top of the filing cabinet. She told herself she wouldn't check her phone again today. Then she pulled it from her pocket once more and stared at the time, dark and silent, on the display. What did she expect? Guys don't call Rachel. It's like some rule of nature or something.

She climbed round a bookcase into the window and set to work with the posters that had arrived with the latest delivery that morning, pulling each one flat and arranging them as backdrops to the books, smoothing her hand over glossy pictures and words on the paper, hanging and securing them with weights so they didn't curl.

With stops for answering the phone and customers' questions, and quiet cups of tea on her own in the back room, it was nearly three o'clock by the time Rachel had finally finished changing the display in the window.

If she stood right in the corner, her shoulder pushed against the glass, Rachel could just about see up Finkle Street. Past the toyshop on the corner, over the cobbles, she could see almost as far as the little café.

She stole some breath into her body. Will was there, looking into shop windows. Rachel's brain delayed the information as if it knew her body would fail and be unable to keep up. Her subconscious would have to hit her with it slowly. There was Will. Awful leather jacket. Baggy jeans. Seed brown T-shirt. She told herself he needed to change those clothes. He had no taste. No desire to look good.

Then she hated the thoughts that were like drops of maternity in her blood. Stems of motherhood. It wasn't how she wanted to think of him. There was Will. Looking into shop windows. Looking for her. Was he looking for her? She felt, in that childish way, that this was no accident. It was destiny. What were the chances of seeing him here while she just happened to be looking out of the window? She played with the idea that just by thinking about him she had made him appear, made his unconscious body move in her direction, unknowingly drawn to her.

Rachel opened the door and stepped out. She called his name and watched as he walked down the cobbled street towards her. He looked startled to hear his own name in the street. Then he smiled quickly, making Rachel think it was no accident that he was there after all, he expected to see her. He walked slowly and calmly towards her, pretending, she thought, to be cool.

He was different to any other boy she'd ever seen. She didn't know why. Rachel used to think there were only about three types of men in the world, and every one she met was a variation on one she'd met before. But Will wasn't.

He leaned against the door, hands in fists in his trouser pockets. "What time do you finish work?" he asked.

"Five thirty."

"I'll give you a lift home if you like."

She looked at her watch. Even that simple, organised action made her feel old. "But it's only three," she said. "What are you going to do round here till then?"

Will shrugged. "Do you want a lift or not?"

Will didn't know Kendal's streets very well. He didn't come into town much. Besides, he hadn't lived here for long. He'd moved to a school here when he had to start studying for his GCSEs – but he didn't remember his school in Manchester.

He walked away from the door of the bookshop and back up the street. He'd parked his van over the main road in a little pay and display car park that was jammed full with tourists. The main road was being wiped fast by cars, taxis and buses and Will had to stand and wait at the pelican crossing for several long, stretched minutes.

It was no coincidence. Did she know that? Had she herself remembered everything she'd said to him? He had. Will knew Rachel thought he wasn't listening the other night and, to be fair, sometimes that was true, but he knew what she'd said. His brain had drawn it from her and let it settle inside him. He'd watched the headlights isolate the windows of her little house as they walked past on their way to his. She'd talked about her neighbours. She was alone. And at some point that night she'd told Will where she worked and what she did to claw together enough money to buy food and raise plants and guinea pigs. He'd held onto that information; kept it and intended to use it.

The traffic wilted on the road and Will walked across with a family – mum, dad, brother and sister. He felt his feet step in time to theirs. Felt that maybe he could meld with them and feel how it was to be part of something like that. A family. How long was it since he'd understood what that was?

He watched as the family stopped outside a newsagent and the boy started asking for an ice-cream. Then the little girl looked at him and it made his organs shrink inside his body. He quickly turned away when the girl's mother noticed he was staring, and rushed back to the car park.

Then he sat in his van in the car park, just watching people go by, thinking about the girl and the family. When it was finally time he drove out and parked the van on the street outside the bookshop and stood with the door open waiting for Rachel.

She slammed the shop door and the bell that was tucked just inside the shop complained loudly. Smiling, she hurried forward and got into the van beside Will.

"Hey," she said.

"Hey."

But that was all he said. There was definitely something about his mood that was different since his visit earlier in the afternoon.

They drove out of Kendal, over the bridge. In the silence there was still something invisible connecting them, like the harmony of a song. The river beneath them was briefly like a bass line laid beneath its unspoken words.

"So, how was your day?" she asked.

"Fine."

She let a long pause go by. Decided there was no time like the present. "I know someone who lives in Manchester," she said. "Did you like it there?"

"Yeah."

"Tell me about it, I've never been."

Will didn't say anything.

"Which part of Manchester did you live in?" she prompted him. "What was your house like?"

And Will desperately wanted to tell her all about Manchester but there was nothing he could tell her. Not yet. Maybe soon.

"Did you ever meet up with your cousins and stuff?" Rachel continued. "I met one of your cousins at the party."

She looked over at him. He was just staring at the road. She didn't even know if he was listening any more. She waited a few more moments and then realised for her own safety that she needed to break the trance she had apparently put him into.

"It's OK, Will," she said. "You don't have to tell me about Manchester if you don't want to. Let's talk about it another time."

In the village Will parked the van on the pavement outside Rachel's house. He stopped and tapped the steering wheel with his fingers. He seemed as if he was about to say something at first, but he stayed silent.

"Thanks for the lift," Rachel said at last.

Will nodded, not looking at her.

Rachel heard other words in her head. Felt them. Moulded them until the sentences were so real she thought maybe she'd already said them. *Do you want to come in? Are you hungry?* But the silence seemed to make it impossible to speak them. Had she done something wrong? Surely not today: she'd hardly even been with him at all.

She felt something fall inside her. *Oh no, not already. It was too soon for him to leave her.*

Rachel got out of the van. He still didn't look at her. Was he upset that she'd been asking him about Manchester? She went down the passage and into her house at the back.

Five minutes later she was sitting at the kitchen table. She looked at six jars of jam which she'd made and sealed at the weekend, heating a basketful of blackberries picked from her own back garden and pouring in water and sacks of sugar. What was she actually going to do with so many of them? She didn't even have one person to give them to.

Her parents had moved away years ago, before Rachel's grandparents died. Rachel's dad was going nowhere in the village. But if they left he could find a job and put his gambling behind him. Rachel wondered if she was something else he wanted to leave behind, another reminder of how he had failed.

She looked at the table, the mess she never seemed to find the time or the inclination to clear up, things she rammed into every available space. Useless things. Things she bought or made which she could only sit and stare at, no idea what they were supposed to be for.

The jam would keep of course, that was the good thing about jam, but this unnatural loneliness, the sickening desperation, would not: an untamed desire for hands, mouth, eyes that were not her own. It would only be worse if he rejected her now.

She realised her stomach was gurgling and she thought about food. It was almost six thirty now. She went into the living room first and switched on the TV. Outside, at the front of the house, she heard an engine begin. It startled her. She moved forward and saw Will turning the van quickly into the road. Had he been sitting there, staring at the road or the dashboard all this time? He hadn't left her yet.

There was something mysterious going on behind his eyes. She didn't recognise it but it only made her want him more. He was so quiet. Such a lullaby. How would she tell this boy what was happening? What was happening to her.

How would she make him understand? He'd hardly spoken to her at all today, but that didn't seem to matter. Who needs words? Still, she would have to tell him somehow. This was the most important thing that had ever happened to her. He had to know that. It was destiny. It was fate.

Blackpool. Fate. Mixed together now like raisins in cake mixture.

Returning now with hindsight, Andrea could see her fate had been written in the Blackpool skyline all along. She could follow it round in circles with the big wheel and see it crash dramatically with each wave on the beach. Why had she come back here? What was she thinking of? Was she testing herself to see if she could still feel any of those hot, body-bursting ripples of lust that had consumed her on the day when she first came here? If she was, it didn't work.

Her first impression was that the pleasure beach is even more of an island of sensory overload today. And seeing it more clearly for what it is now that the lights are brighter, the music louder and everything so much bigger, Andrea can understand better how she lost her way in there.

She's sure there are hundreds of girls doing the same, making the same mistake she made. And Andrea wishes she could barge through the turnstiles and seek them out behind the cafés, in the halls of mirrors, even in the queues for the rollercoaster. But of course, they wouldn't listen, just like Andrea wouldn't have.

And anyway, she's on a mission and the suitcase she pulls along the golden mile is too ridiculously heavy for her to go deviating from her path.

Andrea was beginning now, after all these years, to truly taste her mother's words on her ageing tongue and wince at the strength of them. Why had she never noticed that before?

You know nothing about this lad, Andrea. He only wants one thing. They all do, his type. I know his type. Can't you find yourself a nice young man in the village? A local man. You know where you are with a local man.

But perhaps that had been the problem. Local men offered no surprises. And Andrea always did like surprises. She'd been looking out for the biggest surprise of her life. She'd been willing it to come her way. Something that would knock her from her dainty feet, widen her eyes like the big world and fizz in every cell of her body.

It happened in Blackpool.

That day. Thirty-odd years ago. On a five-hour outing with her friend Vivien. They'd taken the bus at ten o'clock in the morning, giggles scurrying between them, and they'd made a deal that they would each, irrespective of the other, seek out the fullest thrills they could. They got off the bus and stared at Blackpool. It seemed like every inch of the place was filled to the lid with light, sound and possibility.

By two o'clock in the afternoon, Andrea had already eaten her way through slippery chips, cloggy ice-cream, rock splintered with the town, and candyfloss on a stick. She was feeling dangerously nauseous when she sat down in a dodgem car with Vivien. But Vivien was the first to be sick. She hurled her chips and ice-cream from the car, splattering the rubber track and narrowly missing Andrea's bare thigh. The car juddered, its underside slowed by vomit. Andrea shrieked and stood up in the car, staring at her leg below her mini skirt where her skin shunned the flecks of acidic potato. That's when they were rammed. The two lads in the other car split with laughter. Andrea was forced back into her seat by the jolt of the car and Vivien was sick again.

When Andrea stepped out of the dodgem she was faced with the passenger of the other car. He leapt out as energetically as Andrea's father had leapt over the seats in the cinema, and took her hand. He kept her attention while his mate persuaded Vivien away from the track. And Andrea saw the whole of her life ahead of her, in the silent promises of this man's quiet brown eyes flickering in the bright lights.

*

Rachel was still standing in the living room. Still staring at the road outside, after the van. She wondered what her mum and dad would make of Will. It wasn't something she needed to worry about, they'd never have to meet him, but she wondered if they'd be able to accept him. She supposed not, especially her mum. She'd be unable to look into him, to see what Rachel could see. She'd be unable to feel anything.

"And what does he do?" her mum would say. "Gardening? That's not going to pay very much."

Rachel couldn't even consider her mum's reaction to Will's age.

Her dad would be a little easier on it, Rachel thought. He'd weigh the smiles he could see coming from Rachel and he'd place them against all the negatives, and he'd see how important he was. That's what Rachel would like to believe.

She was thinking about her dad, and her gran, and the taut strands of distrust always between the two of them. Even as a child, Rachel could see it. She wondered why it had to be that way. Why parents can rarely accept their children's choices. And she knew there was something in Will that even Rachel's gran and granddad would have found difficult, however many smiles he brought to Rachel.

*

He was running up the road, desperate. Needed refuge from the cold weather. The chapel on the hill. Wasn't it true that they were always open? Wasn't there something about a religious building that said nobody would be denied entrance? The snow sank away beneath his boots as he ran. And he could see the grass and the road and then the steps up to the church, all revealed in each print beneath his footsteps.

He didn't care. Just get inside. Just get away from this incapacitating cold. This ridiculous, unnatural cold. In the middle of nowhere in these conditions? On his own? It couldn't be real.

He put his hand on the swirled gates by the entrance to the church. He thought he could feel the metal through his wet gloves, but it was only the cold. Everything felt cold to his touch. Metal, stone, the air, his own face. The wind was crueller than the tight winding road that had led them up there to this place. A road...? The road that cut between the base of hills and decorated their peaks with black tarmac.

He turned, catching sight of the tops of trees, and the farm buildings down below where hay would be stacked in the warmer months and a sheep dog would doze. Then he felt the open breath between himself and whatever it was he was running away from.

The chapel was open, of course. Light full of grain forcing through the stained glass window. No one inside.

He shook it away this morning. Whatever it was. Dream. Fantasy. Maybe he was going crazy. One thing he knew. He didn't want this in his head, not now. He wanted to fill his head with Rachel. And that's what he would do.

*

Time was passing differently since Will had been with Rachel. He had a new sense of contentment even though he hadn't actually seen her again yet. She'd tried to phone him once, but he was driving, and he couldn't stop the van in time to pick up the call. Then he'd just stared at her name on the display.

When she didn't hear from him she sent him a text message that she worded over and over before she finally sent it, but he'd ignored that as well.

He didn't want to mess it up. He wasn't quite sure how to deal with a girlfriend. It was more like she was a secret, and he felt comfortable with that. One which he could hold inside his own chest while his mother shouted at him to pick up his work boots that shed perfect slices of earth onto the carpet by the front door.

"William! Not again William! How many times? Shift those stinking bloody boots!"

She was still a secret he could feel smiling from his eyes every morning as he caught them red-handed, full of wonder, in the rear view mirror of his van. But the banter of his work colleagues put him off every time he thought about calling her.

He parked the van beside the tin out-buildings, like mini aircraft hangers, and he jumped down onto the muddy path. Looked at his feet. His mother would kill him if he stepped into the house like that. He felt the gentle pull of blame inside him. His brother Martin left an earth-slimed football, straight from the field behind the pub, in the hall for days. Martin could leave a tracksuit top that had been rolled in the wet mouth of a goal on the kitchen table, and no one seemed to say a thing.

"Morning Will."

He looked up. It was Steve, who specialised in tree surgery, walking with a mug in his hand, the legs of his trousers already splashed in dirt. And the boss behind him, stepping from the bright light of the office, in identical clothes, a blue sweatshirt and thick black trousers, and carrying sheets of paper held to his chest. Their heavy boots slipped slightly in the wet earth.

"You're down at Arnside today, Will," the boss said. "House overlooking the water." He looked down at the papers in his hands as if checking the architecture of the house he was sending Will to. "Pretty spectacular it is," he said. "Woman wants the back of the house doing, maintenance work mainly. A doddle."

Will immediately pictured the way the road disappeared into wet earth down at Arnside. How it shifted from stone to moveable ground, to the river, bursting into the sea and going on forever.

"Steve, you're at Penrith," the boss said.

"Bloody hell, that's miles away! It'll take me half the day just to get there."

"I'll do it." Will was aware that maybe he'd jumped in too quickly. Seemed too eager. "I mean, if it's not..." he motioned to Steve. "Long as it's not tree stuff. I don't mind going, if you want to swap."

Steve looked at the boss. His wife hated him being home late. Moaned from the minute he got in to the second they curled into bed if he'd been late. "Suits me," he said.

"Are you sure, Will?" the boss asked. "It's a long drive."

Will was thinking about the water sloshing on the walkway in Arnside again. Wet fingers slapping the cold stone by his feet, and wherever he looked, the sea coming in. He said he was sure. Said he liked driving.

The boss shrugged. "Well, if you're sure." And Steve laid his hand on Will's shoulder and said to the boss, "Aye, it'll be that woman he's got filling his head. Long drive's as good as a cold shower. Ain't that right, Will?"

They both enjoyed watching Will blush to the colour of a deep sunset. And the boss laughed. "You just keep your mind on the road, Will," he said. "A woman like that wasn't meant for romance."

Steve and the boss were there that night at his birthday party, and saw him leave with Rachel. Had ribbed him about it ever since.

They don't know Will still thinks of himself as an item with Rachel, even though he hasn't been in touch with her for two weeks. But he hears their words all the way up the M6 and can't get them out of his mind. He's only twenty-one, his whole life is ahead of him. She is... well, she's thirty-something, he doesn't know quite how old. But she's old. She'll tie him down.

And yet at other times he reminds himself of the spark of jealousy in their eyes. Remembers that although they might crack their jokes, they beg him to describe the arch of her back, the taste of her skin, the way her shoulders are covered in scribble curls when she lets her hair down.

Still, he never quite gets up the courage to call her.

If he could remember something about Manchester, he wouldn't be so worried about ringing her. For two more weeks since that drive to Penrith he has been racking his brains but he can't understand why everything is so blank. Like a void in his memory. Like a black hole in space.

Then the boss asks him and Steve to work a Saturday. Just this once. Overtime pay. And by mid-morning Steve is asking about Rachel again. Steve puts his protective gloves on his hands and picks up his chainsaw.

"You still seeing that woman?" he asks.

Will shrugs.

"Good," Steve says. "You should keep it like that if you ask me." He slips his hard hat onto his head with his free hand and steadies goggles on his eyes and defenders on his ears. He says Will would be a fool to go back to her. Says she'd stop him from being who he is. He starts the chainsaw and Will sees it kick into life. It is only then that Will realises that is exactly what he wants.

*

Will walked from the Spar in the village with a bottle in his hand, the neck slipping in his fingers like the slide of a bow on strings. When he got to Rachel's house, she was still in the back garden, watching the guinea pigs hop over the grass in their hutch-like runs. She would pick one up and stroke it, listen to it purr, kiss it and let it fall from her hands back onto the ground.

Will stood and watched her for a moment, the cold bottle of wine draining from his grasp.

She didn't say anything when she saw him. Not even with her eyes. He showed her the wine. Thought she would appreciate its meaning. Rachel got up from her crouch by the hutch and took it from him. She picked up a thin knife she had on the back step and she pushed the cork deep into the neck of the bottle. There was a sigh as the slight air escaped, the cork left bobbing in the liquid like a forgotten word. She handed it back to Will and simply went to squat with the guinea pigs again.

It wasn't quite the welcome Will had expected. "You OK?" he asked her.

She turned and looked at him. "Oh, I'm fine, Will," she said. "Just wondering where you've been for the last four weeks, that's all. You never called or anything. You didn't return my messages. And then you just turn up again as if you've never been away."

"I haven't been away. I haven't been anywhere."

"You know what I mean."

He went and crouched on the grass next to her. "I'm sorry," he said. "I didn't mean to upset you. I've just been doing some thinking, that's all."

"Thinking? For four weeks? You must have had a lot to think about." There was a slight crack in Rachel's voice. He meant about the two of them, didn't he? He was going to tell her it was over. She carried on looking at the guinea pigs. "Well, go on then," she said. "Tell me."

"Tell you what?"

"You want to finish it, don't you? That's what you mean. That's what you've been doing all this thinking about, isn't it?" She felt sick inside. She was urging him to do it, even though it was the last thing she wanted right now. But it would be better, she thought, if they just got it over with.

She looked up at Will. He was smiling.

"No," he said. "That's not what I mean, silly. No, it's something else."

"What? What is it?"

'You know you asked me about Manchester?"

"So?"

"I can't remember."

"What are you talking about?"

"I know I was born in Manchester, right? But I don't remember a thing about living there. I don't really remember much at all about before we came here. It's strange, that, isn't it? I mean, who doesn't remember their life at all?"

"You must remember something," she said.

He shook his head. "Nope. I've tried, but there's nothing."

She put her hand on his arm. He looked even younger like this. Vulnerable. He needed her. He was telling her his problems, his fears, in a way she knew he had told no one else. She had something to tell him too, but not like this. Tomorrow, she thought. She'd tell him tomorrow.

They stayed in the garden until late, on deck chairs shoved close together. Will had to drink most of the wine himself and when he had finished he left the last of it to dribble into the grass, freeing the bottle on the ground. He left everything as Rachel took his hand and led him into the house.

The next morning Rachel woke up with Will's arm over her chest. He was heavier than she would have thought. Heavier than he looked. She shifted. Wriggled from under his grip. She gently placed his arm back on the empty space her body left behind, and stood in the morning light.

Her bedroom was white, apart from one wall on which Rachel had painted an ocean wave swirling like a black hole of cloud and sky. Two double wardrobes that were once her gran's stood against the wall behind the door. Rachel still didn't like going into her gran and granddad's old room, certain she'd encounter their ghosts, although she'd moved these wardrobes out of there so she could use them.

Rachel could see dust floating in the air, caught in a tube of sunlight that stretched from the window all along the wall to the wardrobes at the back of the room. They'd left the curtains open last night. Too impatient for each other, and besides, no one could see in. She went naked to the window and looked out. Down in the garden blood was streaked over the grass like a smear on a lens. Her sleepy eyes twisted into focus, and Rachel put her hand up to her mouth. There were carcasses lying ripped open on the tip-toe stepping stones in the centre of the garden. They'd left the guinea pigs out all night.

He reached the road and looked up at the two pubs next door to each other. He'd never get served, his pimply fourteen-year-old skin betraying him before he even tried. There were no shops in this... this... village? What was it? – two pubs, a lake, a car park and a chapel on the hill. He walked past the second pub, which had three steps up to the door where tired ramblers would climb, wearily read the notice 'No Walking Boots Inside' and then sit down to unlace their caked boots, with their legs threatening to never get them up again. What was the point? What was the point in walking until your legs ached and your feet were numb? Why did they bother? And so he started running up the hill.

And then a gap.

A void.

Then he's in the little chapel. He's cold. Hugging his own body. His parents haven't come for him. He thinks for a panic-filled moment that his family have forgotten him or maybe just left the village without him because he was being such a pain. He kicks the hand-decorated prayer mat in front of him. Stupid knitted picture of animals and grass and sunshine. Then picks it up to use it as a pillow. He wants to hide from something...

He's already been snooping around, standing on the pulpit, trying out the ancient organ, eyeing up the large font in the big Bible that's open and spread over a brass book stand. But it was something else that had caught his eye, that he was hiding from. Not the stained glass window. Not the cross. Not the candles or the dried flower arrangements. Something else.

Someone...?

Someone had been in the chapel with him. Someone in one of the pubs must have seen him. Had they followed him?

What had they done to him?

Why can't he remember what's in the void?

Rachel woke Will. She was shaking his shoulder. From underneath the blackness of his sleep, he came back up to the surface. Gulped air. He had almost dredged it this time. Whatever it was: the thing, deep down. He was getting closer to retrieving it every time. The tiny, brittle, buried skeleton of a truth.

No doubt he would fish again. Search harder. He would dive. Trawl. Even though he didn't want it: it was something he had purposefully hidden, as deep as he possibly could, safely beneath all the stacked thoughts that his brain worked through at night. All he knew was that there was a good reason for that.

But it was so close this time.

He could feel a force moving his bones. Shaking him awake. He opened his eyes. The room was too bright. He brought his arm over his face and tried to focus on Rachel. She was upset. His brain stopped sorting and delving, and let everything drain away back to the sea. He tried to sit up, his body strangely weak. "What's wrong?" he managed.

Will found a spade in the shed at the bottom of the garden. Its blunt end scraped the stepping stones as he edged the little dead bodies onto it. He was used to this kind of thing. Found he was totally unfazed by any kind of natural animal killing. He would have put the dead guinea pigs straight in the bin, but Rachel insisted he buried them.

She told him they were the closest thing to family she had, so he laid them down in a row next to a rose bush and he began digging. Poor little buggers, he thought. A fox, most likely.

"It might have been bad luck for the guinea pigs," he tried to joke, "but the fox must have thought it was Christmas!" But he felt uncomfortable with the light-heartedness of his words and Rachel turned away abruptly.

So he picked up the spade and put his back into the digging a bit more respectfully. Maybe they *were* like family to her. He noticed Rachel at the kitchen window in the corner of his eye as she wiped a tear across her cheek.

She put two mugs of tea on the rough wooden table. Piles of unwashed clothes balanced on one of the chairs, and a half-eaten packet of biscuits crumbled onto a stack of unopened bills on top of the table. Catching Will eyeing the mess, she quickly scooped the crumbs up into the palm of her hand and threw them into the sink behind her. He would have to get used to this, she thought, if he was staying around. Hopefully, he was tidier than she was. She looked at him and wondered what he'd be like to live with.

The hair around Will's ears looked dark and wet. He wiped his face with his sleeve, dragging it in his fist until he could rub it over his eyes and head. She could smell his work. This was what he did everyday. And yet he didn't look like someone who did so much manual work. Shouldn't he look more muscular? And not so boyish: not so pretty or so feminine.

But then Will pulled his t-shirt over his head, hunching his shoulders and dragging the shirt from the collar in one quick movement, and Rachel could see the bulge of his upper arm where daily spade-work and slabs of paving had built up his muscle. He was still skinny, with narrow hips, and his stomach concave, but he was certainly a man, not a boy. He let his t-shirt fall onto the back of the chair beside the rest of the washing, and sat down. Rachel sat down in the chair next to him and blew on her tea that was too hot to drink.

"I'm pregnant."

No.

"Will did you hear me? I said I'm pregnant."

He put his head in his hands, his elbows on the table. This wasn't happening. He stayed like for a moment, thinking how strange that when he was dreaming he was always wishing things were clearer, wishing he understood what was going on in his dreams. And now that something was real, *very* real, he wished it could be a dream.

"Are you sure?" he said.

"Yes, I'm sure. My period was due three days ago."

"Have you been to the doctor's?"

"Not yet."

Rachel seemed to be angry with him for not saying the right words, but he didn't care at that moment and he clung on to the tip of a possibility. "Then how can you be sure?" he said.

"I've done a test, Will. They are accurate. I am pregnant."

He looked up at her.

"Well, is it mine?"

And the anger was rising up inside her. He could see it.

"Of course it's yours," she said. "What do you think I am?"

His walking is all wrong. His legs, his feet, his knees, his hips. His movements feel misplaced somehow. The way he imagines moving in double gravity would feel. How is it that he can make it up the hill under the weight of all the things in his head now?

The guinea pigs themselves were easy. He'd dealt with things that on the surface were far worse than that. But he had made it harder for Rachel: the look on her face after his stupid joke about the fox. And now his mind was holding onto the sight of the guinea pigs, blood and ripped flesh, that he couldn't let go.

And there was no respite in what Rachel had just told him. She was growing a new family. He, Will, had made something begin inside her. He'd caused a life. He didn't mean to, but apparently, so she said, he'd given her a baby.

Maybe he should be happier than he was. Maybe, when he'd calmed down, he would be happier about it. But he'd been unable to face it at that precise moment. The moment she told him. Her words felt cold and he couldn't answer them. Couldn't face up to it. Had to turn away. And for now, he had to get away: up the hill to his house. His body was feeling strangely alien as it moved along the side of the road.

Rachel was still sitting at the table with her hands warming around the mug of tea. She'd made a mistake. She'd thought... what had she thought? That he could handle this? That he felt the same as she did and saw this as some kind of 'meant to be'?

Outside, the spade was still leaning like a gangly man against the wall. A reminder to her of the grave he'd dug for her closest family. But it made some kind of sense to her: when one life ends, another begins.

He'd offered her no more words, not after 'is it mine?' Nor even looked at her. No eye contact. No contact at all. He'd simply got up and walked out the door.

Gone. Did he think that was it? Was that his way of telling her he was walking out on their relationship?

He couldn't just leave like that, without a word.

She couldn't let him leave her now.

She put her hands down gently on the table and let her fingertips stretch to where his hands had just been. A relationship. The baby meant she did have one of those this time – didn't she? Whatever that was. A connection that held them together even though they were apart.

For the first time, she was sure that she did have that, the one thing she'd been looking for. What her gran and granddad had. They would never have thought of leaving the other. So despite what had just happened, Rachel felt for sure that she now had a relationship. If only she understood how a *relationship* worked.

Rachel pulled Will's t-shirt from the back of the chair beside her. It looked as if it was slipping into the pile of washing, migrating to meet all the other smelly, needy clothes. She would wash his t-shirt and anything else of his. She would become the home-maker she had never been. And it would happen normally and naturally. Because that's the way it had to be.

She held the t-shirt, put it to her face and breathed in.

Walking up the road, nearly at the turn-off to his estate, Will realised he was cold. He put his hands to his arms, his shoulders, his body, and realised it was bare, goose-bumped skin.

Still waiting in the chapel. It was cold. Felt like it was getting colder every second. His family were taking too long to come looking for him. He should at least be able to hear them by now, their boots squelching in the mud and stomping on the path, their voices irritated, frustrated, exhausted, calling for him. But he couldn't hear anything. Silence filled up his head, threatened to split his skull. Something was wrong. Something from the void. Will felt it. Sensed it. Something was very wrong.

He was rubbing his arms. Stepped straight out in front of a car. Heard the horn. Heard the brakes complain. He looked up and saw the scared scowl of the woman behind the wheel. Will ran across to the other side of the road and up to his house.

"What are you doing walking about like that? Where's your shirt?"

Will's dad was on his knees in a kitchen cupboard. His clothes strained across his back and his legs where he bent his wide body. He'd turned around when Will walked in, but stayed hunched awkwardly in the corner. His glasses slipped on his nose and he pushed them back up, the school teacher in him still hard-wired into his movements even though he now had an office job. His other hand was grasping in the corner cupboard for a fresh cloth to wipe away the ball-shaped evidence of Martin's latest football practice.

"Where have you been anyway?" he said. "I know you're old enough now, but a phone call wouldn't hurt, would it?"

Will leaned against the door and watched his dad, bent over in the cupboard. He realised it must be the weekend for his dad to be at home. Felt the shock of not knowing what day it was.

He mumbled to his dad that he was 'seeing' Rachel Murdoch who lived in the end terrace down in the village. One surprise at a time.

"She lives in that last terrace down the hill, you know the one? She came to my party."

He said the last bit lamely, letting his words hang. He wondered if he had needed to tell him which house.

Martin suddenly traipsed into the kitchen with the bucket and sponge he'd been using to wash his much loved car, and making their dad's efforts with the cloth seem useless.

"Then I had to bury her guinea pigs. A fox had 'em, I think. It was a right mess on the garden this morning, all in bits and blood..." Will hadn't really wanted to say that. But he was nervous because he knew Martin had had more girlfriends than him, and he didn't want any of the same kind of comments that he got from his work colleagues.

Fortunately, Martin was too interested in knowing all the details about the guinea pigs to bother teasing Will.

"Were they, like, ripped apart then?" he asked. "Had their heads bit off and stuff?" he laughed. "Gross!"

Will's dad, Ian, eyed Will. "So that's it, is it?" he said. "That's where you've been. That's who you've been with." He stood up, stroked an imaginary beard and shook his head. "Not sure if we should mention this to your mother, you know. Not sure what she'd have to say about it."

Will covered his body with his arms in the doorway. "I'm twenty-one dad," he said. "Anyway, we'll have to tell mum now."

"Why?"

He thanked God his mother wasn't here. He calculated ahead, that it would be easier this way. His dad could tell her and maybe she'd take it better, maybe she wouldn't go as ape as she would if he told her himself.

"Because..." he said. "Because she's going to be a grandma. I'm going to be a dad. Rachel's pregnant."

It sounded weird out loud. Out of his own mouth. But it also sounded real now. Strangely, it sounded like something that was possible. Could this be possible?

Will's brother stumbled in the doorway and sloshed his bucket of water in the sink. 'Bloody hell,' he said.

Will is lying on his bed. Something is put in front of him and snatched away. It happens over and over. Maybe if he could finally see what the thing was... – maybe then at last it wouldn't keep coming back to torture him?

Martin is juggling a football repeatedly on his feet, watching it to make sure it doesn't drop to the grass, his legs blinking in a strange quickened can-can. Will is busy planting bulbs in the subtle earth for his mum. But it is not their garden here in Hilltop.

That must have been about the time he realised it wasn't a chore and he loved doing it. Loved the feel of the sticky earth on his fingers. Loved imagining the moment when the growth silently started deep down where he'd planted it, and eventually announced itself in the stalk and flower. His mum was happy then. She smiled from the back door and called him a good boy.

It was before. Before something had struck her. Everything was different.

The ball eventually skids away from the control of Martin's trainers, and his whole body sags with defeat. And with his face drenched in anger and frustration, Martin hurls the football at the flower bed where Will was planting.

And then what? Will doesn't think the ball hit him. That couldn't cause amnesia, could it? But he feels a tug inside his heart, of a memory that has been lost.

He spends all of that evening lying in his own bed at home. He can hear his mum and dad talking upstairs. He's caused a panic. Something about him and Rachel of course. But it's none of their business. Will has just turned twenty-one. He's been told so many times that he's a man now. There are no more dates like that to reach. He can do anything he wants. Even if he'd never intended doing it.

He closes his eyes. Decides, for the first time, that he wants to bring back the memories. Tries to bring back the memory of him and Martin, to see what else he can remember, but it doesn't work out like that: instead he falls into a doze and wakes with a start from a nightmare about dead guinea pigs.

It makes him think about waking up with Rachel at her house and finding the guinea pigs dead. She'd been upset about that. He would go round to see her tomorrow after work, maybe pick her up again if he could get away early enough. Yes, surprise her. Sit outside the bookshop in his van and wait for her to come out. Tells himself, stubbornly, that he doesn't care what anybody says. The idea of the baby had started to shift inside of him. It began to bake.

*

It's Wednesday. He still hasn't been to surprise Rachel at work yet. But he has found out from his boss that he has to go back to Penrith tomorrow and stay over to finish the work off on Friday. So if he doesn't go into Kendal today, maybe he never will.

The sky is clear this evening. The days are getting longer. Will is sitting in his van. Window open. Arm resting on the door. Smiling. He watches her come out. Sees the boss toss her the keys and then hurry up to the Italian restaurant for a date; Rachel twisting the bundle of keys in the door. Will is smiling at this lily flower in a dirty puddle. Will reaches forward and turns the volume down on his radio as Rachel approaches the van.

"Oh, it's you," she says. "You left your stuff the other day when you walked out."

Will's smile retracts. He opens the door of his van and gets out. "What?"

"Your t-shirt. Did you walk all the way home like that? You must have been freezing."

He just looks at her.

"And your cap," she says. "Haven't you missed that at work this week?"

"Oh yeah." He points behind him at the van. "Do you want a lift? I came to give you a lift home."

She'd intended being so angry. As soon as she had seen the van parked outside, she had been rehearsing her anger. Will had walked out on her three days ago in the middle of a life-changing conversation and hadn't been in touch since: how could he now turn up again, smiling ridiculously, as if nothing had happened.

She should be angry.

But now, standing there in the flesh with him, she couldn't

make those words work in her mouth.

He really did not appear to understand what had happened at all. How could he be like that? Surely something isn't right. This couldn't be the way it's supposed to be.

"OK Will," she says, getting into the van with him. "But no more walking off like that, all right?"

She looks at him for an answer, but he's blank. She feels like his bloody mother. Will nods, and turns the key.

He reminds her of a wild rabbit she used to keep at her granddad's allotment. She hadn't gone looking for it. It had come to her, almost asked to be taken in. As if it didn't want to be wild anymore. And then she hadn't been able to send it away again: she just feared for it, how it would cope alone in the open fields.

*

Andrea tucked the teddy bear under her arm as she walked up the street to her house. Felt the secret in her skin, the mystery that all the girls giggled about but that she had now discovered; a secret she wouldn't tell, the lie, if she needed it, already spoken in her head. She twisted her heel on the uneven path in the alley, steadied herself with her hand against the damp, black walls, and walked, a changed, opened person, into the little terrace where she lived.

Her mother, Mary, propping up the extra leaf of the table to make it bigger, ready for their tea, could smell the shame as her daughter walked through the door.

"What have you been up to?" she asked.

Andrea was fiercely tugging on the hem of her mini skirt, too aware of her knees and the expanse of thigh above them.

Mary watched her from the edge of the table. "It's no use trying to make it any longer now," she said. "Should have thought of that earlier. It's a good job your father can't see you." Then she sighed and years of frustration were free in the air for a moment. "What have you been up to today?"

"Nothing."

"Nothing? So you and Vivien did nothing?"

Mary felt an argument coming that was already destined to happen and there was nothing she could do to stop it growing inside her. She wanted to stop it. Why couldn't she stop it?

"We went to Blackpool. I told you," Andrea said, taking another teasing bite of the candy floss.

Mary eyed the teddy bear under Andrea's arm.

"Hmm. Suppose you've been with a lad," she said.

"Mu-um."

"Well, have you?"

Andrea was thinking about the boy. She could feel his presence still all over her skin.

"I did meet somebody," she said.

Mary threw her hands up in the air as if giving thanks. Andrea almost expected a *Hallelujah!* to come flowing from her mouth.

"Oh heaven help us," she said instead. "Not some fairground lad. For goodness sake, Andrea."

"No, no, he's not. He's not from Blackpool. He was there for the day like us."

"So where is he from then?"

Andrea thought for a moment. Between the kisses and the long silent staring at her future in his eyes, she hadn't thought to ask him where he was from. It didn't seem to matter while she was holding his hand and leaning her head against him, or even when they slipped easily behind the haunted house, the ghostly moans mingling with his own as Andrea discovered, at last, what it was all about where men and women were concerned.

'I don't know," she murmured.

She knew all she needed to know, she thought. She knew about his fingertips. Knew how it felt when he rubbed against her. Knew about his eyes and all that she saw in them. Why the fuss?

"You don't know?" Mary started to set the table in the kitchen, almost throwing the cutlery onto the pressed white cloth and dealing flowered plates down as if throwing in her hand at cards.

"Oh our Andrea," she said. "You're priceless, you are."

*

"Can we stop down at the shops first?" Rachel asked.

The van curled round the dual carriageway and dipped under hooded trees. They passed a stately home that Will always wondered about as he drove past: the clothes, the ways, and the speech of the long dead people who once lived there. And now he was entering a world as alien as that to him.

He nodded at her. "Of course."

Rachel stared at the windscreen. There was a great arc of clear glass where the wipers had pushed all the muck and grime aside into the corners that were almost brown. As much of a contrast as there was in Will now. It was as if the person Rachel had given her mind-blowing news to on Sunday had been transformed into this other, similar person, who could take it all so much better.

He didn't even seem, dare she believe, as if he was unhappy about it all. She turned her head and looked at him. He was smiling. In front of her the sky was blue.

"We should go out somewhere on Saturday," Rachel said. "It's my weekend off. I know, we should go down to Morecambe Bay. I went there once with mum and dad when dad was—" She turned and looked at Will again. She hadn't spoken to him about her parents. He had never asked and she hadn't sensed the right time to tell him yet.

Will was watching the road. He was blinkered. He wasn't listening.

"Well," she said. "We should get out together anyway. Doesn't really matter where we go. Do you want to?"

She looked at him until the way he ignored her sent a ghost of a feeling through her body. Then she looked away too. Both of them silent again. She couldn't stand it if he rejected a single one of her words.

*

Before the void there was warmth in their family. Banter in their car journeys.

They'd set off early from home. Will had helped to carry the bulky cases to the car, placing each one snugly in the boot. Even though he was fifteen, beginning to feel the burdensome weight in his mind of doing things like that. Helping his parents, carrying cases, doing dishes, anything. It wasn't what a teenager did.

"...we'll be able to get out into the open much more often. We'll be able to do things like this as a family all the time. I tell you kids, you'll never want to go back to a city again once we live out here."

*

The van cleared the hill beside the houses where Will lived and slowed down at the crossroads. They turned into the village square, parking the bulky van where market stalls would be propped against one another once a week.

In the village people are looking at them. He's holding her

hand. She's smaller than him, no matter what her age dictates, and she's small, beautiful. He has walked like this with a girl before, a girl smaller than him, like Rachel is. He has irrational, unwanted need to protect her and care for her, to look after her. It's something he knows he has felt before, but doesn't know when. And it makes him feel disloyal somehow.

Will tries to smooth the frown away from his face. Neighbours, who spread gossip like poppies in a field, look at Will and Rachel with pity as they stare from the doorway of the butcher's shop, the pained hooves of pigs mounted by their heads. They whisper with spite, even some anger. But the baby is still invisible. How do they know?

Will can tell the baby has affected everything. It has made Will and Rachel walk the streets hand in hand, and it has set a confusion in Will's body like a continuous current in the sea, and yet it isn't something that is colouring their skin or is in any other way obvious. So how do they know?

At home it's made his mum cry and shout, and his brother smirk, and made his dad take their side against Will. Out in the village square it's another reason to look down on Will. And it seems to have given people another reason to hate Rachel, as if they needed one. This baby is no bigger than a grain, but it's changed Will's whole life already.

They walk past the hairdressers and Will suddenly realises how they all know.

His mum had an appointment there today. And she was there long enough to have her hair washed, rinsed, and washed again. Long enough to forget what made him her son at all.

He can see her now, at the bakery, where all the ladies gossip in the queue. At the greengrocer's, shaking her head along with the neighbours at someone else's son. Having tea in the little café with her hateful words.

A woman emerges from the teashop, and stumbles on Will and Rachel together. She forces a sugary smile. "William. Hello love. How are you these days? I hear..."

And her words trail into nothingness as she looks quickly away. She'd heard, of course, that Will's girlfriend was up the duff. She'd heard that Rachel was a good ten years older than him and what a mess he'd got himself into this time.

Will's mum always did try to make out that the way he had been as a boy meant she couldn't do anything for him now. Despite his laziness, Will would always do as he pleased. Will was a law unto himself. She always said things like that. And now she would be carrying on as if Will was nothing to do with her at all. Judging another mother for letting *this* happen.

He looks at Rachel who hasn't seemed to notice. Or doesn't care. And he follows her into the shops. Rachel buys bread at the Spar, two ready meals from the freezers lined up in the middle of the shop, and shampoo and black boot polish that Will knows will stand on the side in her kitchen for days, maybe weeks, before Rachel decides what to do with it.

Rachel pays for her shopping. Will is still watching her as they get back in the van. He knows he is feeling a strange emotion that he hasn't felt for some time.

They drive up, out of the village square, past the pub where Will had his birthday party, the road where he first held her hand, and they park outside Rachel's house. She drops the bags back in the kitchen and runs cold water onto her hands, which she then splashes on her face.

Will thinks about asking if she feels sick or something. If she's all right. Then he lets the words drain away from him. He doesn't want to hear the answers. He feels everything ballooning around him. He doesn't have any control. He has to regain some control. Rachel and the baby are changing everything.

Will knows there is a certain path he's supposed to go down now. Be responsible. Be a father. Live with Rachel and this baby. Maybe even get married. It all seems inevitable.

"I suppose you'd better meet my mum and dad," he says.

Rachel opens cupboards, putting the things away. Doesn't look at him yet. He wants her to meet his mum and dad.

It would have to happen some time, she thinks. She is having Will's baby. Might as well happen now. She builds the moment up in her head when she will meet his mum. And she thinks about how strange it will be. The last time Rachel was in that house she was hiding from Will's mum on the floor, now she was going to have to face her.

"Do you want me to?" she asks.

Does he? Does he really want to do this? He thinks about his mum's face when he walks in with this woman she hates before she's even looked into her eyes. And he wants to make her see what he has with Rachel, that they are a couple, and see if she still treats him like a lame kid. He wants to show that he does know what he's doing here. He wants to make himself believe that.

"Well, you should, don't you think?" he says. "They are going to be grandparents."

Rachel likes the sound of those words. They push spy holes in the air and Rachel feels she can look in on how ordinary people do this. Grandparents. Could she acquire an alternative pair of grandparents, by proxy? It's as if he's offering her something. She crumples the plastic bags and slips them into a drawer.

"OK," she says.

Will leaves the van parked outside Rachel's house and they walk up to Will's. He bends his head to admire the van as they walk. A statement, tilting on the curb, of something he has, something he owns and has worked for, that no one, not even his mother, can take from him.

The path at the top of the hill borders Will's house and garden. It's the first house. Number 1. The garage slots in beside the kitchen, but with two cars and a van in the family, Will has never parked in the garage. It's the first time Rachel has seen the house in daylight. The first time she's seen it at all since *that* night.

Will pushes the door and leads her inside.

"Mum, this is Rachel," he says.

Rachel marks the tone of his words. He doesn't talk to his mum as if he feels any discomfort at all. No embarrassment at introducing Rachel to her. No awareness of how awkward this meeting could be. Rachel thinks that's certainly not the way she would be if she was introducing him to her mum and dad.

Will appears so detached. He doesn't carry any of the arguments they must have had in his youth forward to the present, nor any leftover hatred from his adolescence. It's almost as if they aren't related at all. He seems to talk to her as if she is simply a person. Any person.

His mum is standing in the kitchen. "Yes." She says it as if she's confirming something for Will. She starts getting washing powder out of the cupboard. Her back is turned.

She's a small woman, but hard, stern. Rachel can see that. The men in the house tower over her head like sunflowers, and she has to make herself tougher every day. She's getting less of the light as the boys grow, and as her husband grows a middle-aged spread.

Rachel doesn't even notice that Cath looks away as Will's dad comes through to the kitchen. Doesn't know Cath resents him for uprooting them and bringing them here, and that she considers it to have been the biggest mistake of their lives.

But Rachel does see Cath roll her eyes slightly as Will grabs his dad with words, a bond of testosterone Cath can't break. "You remember I was telling you about Rachel...?"

"Ah, yes. Hello love." Ian passes Rachel with his hands on her shoulders. And he is obviously an even softer version of Will. An older, mellower version, calm and grounded here amongst the hills and the deep lakes.

Rachel notices then how Will becomes a little boy around his parents. He slides back five years, maybe more, and Rachel suddenly feels that the gap between the two of them is wider, like an animal trap opening up in the ground.

Will's mum is doing his washing, stuffing his underpants into the drum with his eggshell shirt, bunching them together and never looking at them, not understanding what these things mean now, not able to smell the sex on his pants and the spread of sweat on the arms of his shirt, not noticing the way the collar is pulled to one side, or that the button holes are stretched, where Rachel has pulled at his clothes; taken the boy his mum and dad made and turned him into something else.

"And then there's our Martin," Will was saying. "I think maybe you met at my party." Will takes Rachel into the living room. "Martin, Rachel's here."

Martin looks up from his PlayStation. His eyes blink an out-of-reach recognition at her, and his teeth shine in his smile. "All right?" he says.

Rachel is smiling at Will's brother now.

"Hello Martin." Rachel says his name precisely as if her tongue can't cope with the feel of it in her mouth. As if she's never heard a name like that before.

Will's seen something in his brother's eye. He's smug, of course, because he's never got a girl pregnant like Will. Especially not one who's more than ten years older than himself. And he doesn't have to sit round the table in the mornings while his mum says, *we've nothing against her. I'm sure she's very nice. It's just that, well, maybe she's ready to settle down and have a family, but you... you're only young yet and I, we, we're not so sure you're ready for this. You're too young to be settled like that. You're too young.* Then she sighs and holds up her hands again as if she's remembered how fragile her relationship with Will is. And Will's dad stares at her when she says, *I don't care. Do what the hell you want, but don't do it here. Don't do it anywhere near me.*

Martin's concentration never wavers from the PlayStation but he is thanking God it isn't him in Will's place. Even while he laughs at Will on the inside, he can't ignore the fact that it could have been him instead. He knows these things happen.

Accidents happen.

She turns away quickly and moves over to the window. Begins touching things. Photos. One of Martin when he bought his first car from the wages he saved as a mechanic, leaning against the doors, arms folded. One of Will, years ago, standing at a poolside, dripping wet, wearing black speedos and goggles on his head like idle sunglasses, holding up a medal.

"What's this?" Rachel asks.

"Oh yeah," says Will. "Apparently I used to be something of a swimmer."

She inspects the picture closely, even loving this other, adolescent Will who she's never known. She feels the loss of not having him in her life when she was that age, and the jealousy of his years without her.

Her eyes move swiftly over to the picture of Martin, older, more confident. She vaguely recognised something of Will in this photo as well, and wondered how much the boys had looked alike when they were younger.

"Aren't there any of you two as kids?" she asks.

She looks over at Martin who has looked up urgently from his game, a black warning on his face.

Will says, unsure, "Er... no. I don't think so."

He looks at Martin too, and Martin's face tries to hide its panic. He shakes his head now. "Never seen any," he says. "Probably lost when we moved."

Rachel can see the shining edge of a secret. Sharp. She looks away. It's a secret Martin has deep in every bit of him, and Will doesn't seem to have at all.

Will's mum shouts from the kitchen, "Tea or coffee?"

And Will turns away from the photos and shouts back. "Oh no mum, Rachel's not having any caffeine. It's bad for the baby."

There's a silence before his mum pushes the door and walks in with a tray of cups and jugs, a teapot, sugar bowl and tea spoons; a silence where Martin's panic fades and Will remains oblivious. Cath sets the tray down, says, "You can see to it then, William. Don't think I'm messing about making different bloody drinks," then turns to walk out again. At the door she stops. There's a sudden feeling in the room. The air cold. "And don't think I haven't noticed either," she says. "What you've been doing to my plants."

Will looks at her. A pale look. Hollow, and pale as the winter sky.

"Bloody spiteful, it is," Cath says. "And you, you're supposed to like the things." She points a trembling finger at him. "You'll kill all my plants as well now, will you?"

She slams the door and Will looks with embarrassment at Rachel, touches her arm. He decides to wait for a while before he offers to get her a glass of water. When he turns back he sees Martin dip his head, a smile bleeding onto his face now.

The moment, that had stuck in the air, begins to disperse like soda bubbles. She had to ignore them. Ignore the situation. What the hell was that all about? Killing plants? What? Rachel thinks for a minute that maybe she had been better off when she didn't get too close, didn't get involved. This situation was so tightly packed it was squeezing the breath out of her.

Rachel pushed her nose up to the window. Wanted to get out of here, but it wasn't an option any more. This could be her family. Her new family: what she'd wanted. But they were even worse than her own, absent parents. It was all a lie. There was no such thing as a happy family, was there?

She touched her stomach. She would make a new one. Never mind her own parents or this family. She would make one that was different. Special. Untouchable.

She looked out of the window. Saw that there was washing on the line in the next garden, thrashing in the wind. Rachel wondered what they were like next door, whether they were new to the area: people round here hardly ever put their washing out, as the sky was forever watching, bubbling with black clouds or sheeted in dulled chrome.

The neighbour came out, holding a baby in one arm, and an empty laundry basket in the other. A picture of Rachel's future? The baby inside her would be born and she would be expected to become this other person, adding a baby to the juggling of everything else she had always done.

She wanted to think that she and Will would easily slip into the mould, that being a proper family wouldn't be out of the question. It was what she had always wanted. She could build the thing she'd been missing.

But how would that work with Will? For the first time in ages she missed her mum. Wanted to ask her about bringing up a baby. And she realised she hadn't thought this through. Hadn't allowed her mind to stretch out to the time in the future where there would be another, dependent, person.

Will kept looking at her while he poured tea from the old

stainless steel teapot, obviously a hand-me-down from a generation before – nobody owned teapots like that any more. Rachel smiled a reassurance at him. "It's OK," she said, looking at the empty cup in front of her. "I'll have a weak one. It won't hurt."

Sitting by the window, Will was staring out, trying to ignore the photo that Rachel had been looking at beside him. The boy by the pool, holding up the medal, the strong competitive swimmer, terrified him now. Blotting it out, he stared at the other gardens through the window.

The one next door and the one next to that were almost identical to the one at the bottom of the hill. He wondered if the people who lived there had looked from their windows and followed suit one after the other, or whether they'd been digging simultaneously, not noticing until they'd stopped and held their lower backs, amazed to see they were shelving their gardens identically.

The man from the bottom house was in his garden now, hacking away at the branches of a tree with a bread knife. Will was about to say something, *look at that idiot, trying to prune his tree with a bloody bread knife!*

But he just stops himself in time as it is only Martin in the room with him.

Will realises Rachel has gone into the kitchen. He can hear her helping his mum with the washing up now. Pots bang on the sink, dull like a knock on bone, waking him out of his trance. Will thinks he has heard his mum ask Rachel why she wasn't on the pill.

Martin looks up from his PlayStation. Will feels the pit of his stomach ache as he sees Martin laughing at him.

"You tool," Martin says, and then starts another game on his screen.

Will ignores Martin and concentrates on the conversation in the kitchen. He can hear his mum saying, "I'm sure you're a very nice... person, but well, our Will, he's quite a bit younger than you isn't he? And what about all your friends, I mean, you two hardly have a lot in common, do you? Are you going to go out with Will and his friends?"

She dipped her voice then. And Will could almost feel the lilt of his mum's head. "Not as if he's got any, but... is he going to go out with yours? Although I suppose with a baby you won't be going out much at all will you? I don't think either of you have thought about this and, you know Will is... Will is..., well you might have done all your living and be ready to settle down with a family, but our Will's only twenty-one—"

"I know how old he is," Rachel said.

From the window it sounded like a sudden tense of brakes. A full stop. And Will respected her for it.

He'd tried to ignore her suggestion about a day trip. Felt it was too big, the question, the idea, all too much too soon. Going away together. Like a proper couple. Especially because she wanted to go to the coast. To the sea, where the sight of the water goes on forever.

But now he listened to her words echoing in the silence in the kitchen and he felt how powerful they were. As if, for the first time, someone was taking him seriously. And he thought, sod it, he could do it. Forget how much it frightened him. He could do this. He would take her on Saturday.

When Rachel went home that evening she made cheese scones and a leaning Victoria Sponge cake which she dusted with soft, cloud-like icing sugar and dented slightly in the centre with a single pebble of a cherry. She looked at the scones, dripping with melted, set cheese, and hoped they would keep until Saturday. If not, she could always make some more. She considered, briefly, taking them back up to Will's and giving them to his mum. Some kind of peace offering: after all, she would more or less be the woman's daughter-in-law. But she couldn't point that fact out – it would be like poking a snake in the eye, and the stupid woman wouldn't take the scones anyway.

So she decided to pack them in pillowy kitchen paper, like her mum had done sometimes when Rachel was small and they'd gone and sat by the swings, or walked down to the next village and hiked up through the trees. She remembered the dark, ancient slope to the stones called the fairy steps, where they had always eaten their picnics there in silence, with her mum dangling her legs from the stones and staring into the distance, over the lapping fields, to other versions of life, to whatever was out there.

Rachel folded the soft paper under each scone. She cut the cake and laid slabs of it down in a plastic box, curling the edges of the tissue paper over the triangular pieces of cake.

On Thursday she and Will had been on the phone to each other all evening. That was how it was meant to be. Rachel was finally worrying about her phone bill: that was what was meant to happen when you had a boyfriend.

12.30 on Friday night. They had made a deal. A secret that was as precious to Will as the night Rachel lay on the floor next to the wall, and hid while Cath came in.

It all seemed a bit over the top and Rachel couldn't see why they didn't just sleep at her house, but she went along with it for him.

On Wednesday Cath had told Will that Rachel could not, under any circumstances, stay over. She said she'd like to say he couldn't see her at all, but she understood how impossible that was, with the baby. She made a face that told Will, without question, Cath thought Rachel had done that on purpose.

"Of course you'll have to be involved," she'd said. "I know that. But just you remember, because she's gone and got herself pregnant doesn't mean you have to stay *with* her. Obviously, you'll be a dad..." she paused there as if she was considering the same question Will had asked Rachel when she told him she was pregnant, *is it mine?* "...but don't go getting any stupid ideas. I know that's hard for you, Will, but try not to act too stupid. Don't make this situation any worse than it is. Just because you're the father doesn't mean you have be with her in any other way."

Will said nothing. He just realised he had a point to make. An inverted, unseen point.

So now Rachel was waiting at the back of the house as her part of the deal. Will's mum wouldn't know she was staying the night, and early in the morning, before anyone else was up, they would drive to Morecambe, as they had already planned.

But Will didn't want to leave the city. This was a stupid excuse for a holiday.

Will covered his ears with his bobble hat, pulling the sides down with tightly gloved fingers. He was trudging with his family in front of him, their boots crunching the freezing mud and flicking specks of it up onto his trousers.

This was a nightmare. At the front of the group, his mum and dad tried to walk hand in hand, but the path was too narrow and it made them almost skip, their feet forced sideways in a hideous sort of dance. They persevered. It was unwatchable. It was ridiculous.

Less than a quarter of the way around the track Will stopped walking. He stared at the still lake, ice in patches like stubborn, scattered thoughts. Slow ripples travelled over the open areas of the water, made by a bird or the fall of a berry from a tree. It must have been several minutes before they realised he wasn't behind them.

"Come on William!" he heard his dad calling. But he just stood there out of sight and waited.

And yet no one came. It was unbelievable. They were carrying on without him. So Will turned away and slouched back the way he had come, his woollen hat almost down over his eyes, his body heavy and slow with too much clothing.

He followed the beaten track back towards the car park, passing someone going the other way. Will hesitated. Wanted to shout, "Don't bother! There's nothing there!" as the person headed for the lake Will had just abandoned. But his face was too cold to move, his mouth too lethargic to speak.

Will's dad had kept on talking about moving here, the house

he'd seen and was going to put an offer on. Would they be expected to do this kind of thing all the time? Will hoped not. When he got to his brother's age, Will thought, he wouldn't do anything he didn't want to any more.

They sleep until five o'clock, curled together in the single bed. Will has set his alarm clock and he lays a finger on it immediately to silence it. They get up and dress on tip toes.

Rachel pulls on her jeans and t-shirt and looks at Will, wondering how she could expect this boy to take on the responsibilities her body will bring. He isn't even planning to delay long enough for some breakfast. She tells Will there's a good chance she'll be sick if she doesn't get some food, and he turns away from her, bending to get his trainers from the wardrobe, a grimace setting on his face.

"OK," he says. "Don't worry, we'll stop on the way."

He realises, behind his reaction, that he shouldn't be thinking about the horror of her being sick in the van, and what he'd do about it, the cleaning up, the mess, the smell. He knows he should be trying to imagine how she must feel.

They leave by the French doors in Will's bedroom, out onto the back garden, and they follow the path around the house to the drive at the front where they get into the van.

As Rachel gets in and closes the door she sees a mutilated lily in the kitchen window with almost all of its petals snipped back closely to the centre of the flower. She looks sharply at Will. "Why *do* you do that?" she asks.

Will starts the engine. "What?"

"The flowers. The lily there, look, in the window. Why do you want to spoil them like that? I don't get it. I thought you loved plants and stuff."

Will glances at the lily in the window above the kitchen sink.

"You think I did it?" he asks in disbelief.

"Well that's what your mum said, isn't it? And you didn't deny it."

"It's Martin. He does it. I've seen him."

"Martin? Why? So why don't you say something? Why do you let your mum think it's you?"

Will backs the van out of the drive. He shakes his head while he moves the vehicle and checks the mirrors. "He's only trying to get a reaction. Stir things up. That's what he's like. He thinks it's funny. He loves getting me into trouble. It's better to ignore him. Don't give him the satisfaction."

"But why would your mum think you did it?"

She stares at him while he breathes the words from his body but doesn't speak them, *my mum hates me, can't you see that?*

"Just leave it," he says. "It's not worth it."

"But your mum said... that's what she was talking about, isn't it? She thinks it's you—"

"It's nothing," he says. "Me and Martin... well, he's always doing things like that. He thinks he's this big joker. Always playing tricks and stuff, you know." Then he shrugs and seems to hear the self-pity in his own voice. "It doesn't matter," he says.

Will winds his window down when they come off the motorway, the blast of cold air circling the cabin until it begins to rain slightly and he can feel the moisture filling his eyes and falling from his face, and he winds the window up again quickly.

Rachel sits with a map on her knee, tracing the roads they should take with her finger on the page.

"Have you been down here before?" she asks him.

"Don't think so," he says.

"Don't think so? Well, don't you know?"

Will shrugs. "No. I mean I don't think I've ever been down

here, no."

Rachel is quiet for a minute, then she says, "What you told me, Will, about not remembering Manchester."

"Yeah?"

"Well, haven't you asked your mum about that? I mean surely she can tell you."

Will sighs and says, "Rachel, me and mum, we don't exactly talk. You must have noticed."

"You could still ask her."

"I'm not asking her anything. She wouldn't tell me anyway, or else she'd tell me a pack of lies."

"Why would she do that?"

He shakes his head. "Just leave it, Rachel."

"OK, but I can't believe you don't remember anything. What about your old friends and things? School friends? You must remember people you grew up with. What about girlfriends? You must have known girls, don't you remember them?"

Will doesn't answer. He tries to think about girls he might have known before they moved here. Their shape. Their faces. Their smell. There was a girl, wasn't there? But he's not sure. He can't pin her down. Can't see her properly. Can't remember what he did with her.

He feels a familiar frustration at not being able to see easily into the past in the way other people can. Glances quickly at Rachel and sees she is still staring at him, waiting for an answer. He looks back to the road. "Are we still on the A6?" he asks. "We should be coming off soon, shouldn't we?"

They park away from the front in Morecambe, amongst the shops. But Rachel gathers their bags and coats and leads Will directly to the open space where the sky meets the land.

The sea is far from the road at Morecambe Bay. Far over the mud flats, where Rachel remembers being plastered from head to foot in muddy sand like wet cement when she was a kid, her dad looking at her hopelessly and then running with her all the way to the ocean's edge, cleaning her off, only to let her fall into the muddy stuff again. She remembers, in a dreamy, untouchable way, how he had dressed her carefully, back on the promenade, dusting the sand from her skin and hanging a loose beach dress with spaghetti straps from her sun-touched shoulders. Then left her with her mum while he disappeared for the rest of the day. Swallowed by the slot machines like their feet in the quicksand.

There are parts of the ground here, she tells Will, that will literally swallow you up if you stand in one place for long enough. It covers your feet and drags you down. The pull of the earth frighteningly strong. She doesn't tell him how terrifying the pull of the slot-arcades can be.

Rachel leads Will down the steps and onto the beach. They take their shoes off on the last piece of concrete and then hold them like little sprigs of flowers in their hands.

"It isn't really a beach," Rachel explains. "But it's the closest you'll get in Morecambe."

They stand on the squelchy ground and Rachel points out to the sea.

"Let's go for a walk before the tide comes in," she says.

Will is looking around him at the wide land, making sure that the sea is only an abstract idea. He tells himself it's safe like that. An idea can be ignored. As long as he isn't looking at it. An idea can be forgotten.

Then he glances at Rachel. He realises she wants to go all the way down to the water's edge. "You don't really want to walk out there, do you?"

"Yeah. You can't come to the seaside and not have a paddle."

Rachel tries to pull him over the mud towards the sea but he resists. It's as if he suddenly has the look of someone stuck at the top of a high fire escape, too scared to move. She tugs gently at his arm. "Will?"

He looks in her eyes. She sees him struggle and try to ditch something in his mind, leave something aside, and then smile. And he runs with her, his big feet leaving liquid craters that fill immediately after his imprint has left them behind.

The sea is calm. When they get there, eventually, it moves quietly like a sheet. Will has stopped. He stands at the shore looking at anything except the water. The sea is a hole in the ground. A huge grave. He's sure he's seen something move beneath the dying waves. An arm. A foot. An open eye.

"Come on," Rachel says.

But Will shakes his head and holds his arms around himself. "I bet it's cold," he says. "And full of seaweed."

"Don't be daft, Will. You're only putting your feet in. Come on." She takes his hand, but he pulls it away from her.

"No, I don't like it, Rache."

"Will," Rachel says firmly. "You don't need to be scared of the water! You're the big swimmer, remember."

"*Was*," he mumbles. "*Was* a swimmer. But it's dangerous here if you're not careful. You know, people get caught out because the tide comes in so quickly and... I've heard about that happening." He turns away and starts walking back.

"Will," Rachel calls after him. "Are you serious Will? It's only a paddle."

He walks all the way back to his van in the car park without Rachel being able to catch up. When she gets back to the road she dusts off the soles of her feet and pushes her wet, gritty toes into her trainers, and then she runs after him.

He is sitting in the van with his legs sticking out beneath the door, his big bare feet exposed on the tarmac.

"Will! What's the matter?"

He is rubbing his feet, fingers working in between his toes.

"Nothing," he says.

"What was all that about then?"

"Didn't want to stay on the beach, that's all. And you shouldn't either. It's too dangerous."

"Well, do you want to do something else? We could find a café or something. I've brought us some scones and cake. I made them myself."

She can hear her own words and they sound ridiculously old, but Will doesn't seem to think so.

"OK," he says, "I am getting a bit hungry."

He stands up and leans on the door, which seems to buckle against his body.

"There's a café over there, look." He points across the road. "We could get fish and chips if you want. Then have your scones."

He smiles at her and takes her hand to lead her over the road to the café.

On the way they pass a sign advertising boat trips. Will ignores it. He thinks Rachel would enjoy that, but he doesn't say anything. He doesn't realise Rachel has also seen it, but when they go to watch the tide coming in, she is not surprised when he takes her back to the beach by a different route.

*

She went back to him that same night. She waited until it was late, dark like the sea under a hidden moon, and she followed the road up the hill to the house. No.1.

The garden that falls from the back of the house grows right up to Will's bedroom. Rachel stepped onto the wet grass. The security light came on and she ducked close to the wall, put her hands on the French windows at Will's bedroom and pressed her face right up to the glass. She tapped with her fingers. Nothing. She turned her hand into a fist and knocked gently. She felt him stir. Rachel knew the way Will woke up, always slowly, always reluctantly. Is there something in his head when he sleeps, she wondered, that he doesn't want to leave behind when he wakes? What does he dream about?

She knocked again, louder this time. A couple of minutes later the curtains at the French doors opened. Will frowned. Felt for the key on the chest of drawers to his left. Unlocked the door and let her in. He went straight back to his bed while Rachel locked the door behind her. She thought about the night he made her lie on the floor while his unsuspecting mum came in to say goodnight. She remembered that was the night the baby began.

Rachel got undressed and got into the bed beside Will. She slept.

Is he crying? She doesn't want to open her eyes for a moment. She can hear something. She can feel him shake. Is Will crying?

"Will?" she whispers.

"Rachel. Is it you, Rachel?"

"Of course it's me. Who else would it be?"

"I don't know."

In the dark everything can seem strange. She thinks, as she puts her arm over his shoulder, how different things feel in the night.

"What's wrong, Will?" she asks.

His body shakes again, and he says, "I'm scared."

"What of?"

"I don't know. Something. I've done something, I know I have. It was my fault."

"I don't understand, Will. What was your fault? What's wrong?"

His muscles tense as if he's seen something in the dark. "You have to help me," he says. "I can't remember. It's like everybody else knows what I've done, but they won't tell me. I dreamt that the police are after me. Do you think they really are?"

"Will, you're scaring me." Rachel has a sudden, strange thought about the last boy she casually took to her bed. All that time ago. How he had frightened her for a second in the middle of the night with his talk about murder and the body in the lake. She felt like she was back there and she could see the same boy in the bed now. The same face.

"What is it, Will? What have you done?" She can feel the strangeness of Will's inability to remember his life suddenly creeping on her. It isn't normal. What had he done that was so terrible? Why does he think the police would be after him? What is he afraid of? Whatever it is, it seems as if it has taken up the whole of his childhood and adolescence, right up until he moved here to The Lakes. Not only does he not know himself, but Rachel realised *she* doesn't really know him at all. He could have been in prison for all she knows.

She looks at him in the darkness. "Will," she says. "You can tell me. What is it?"

"I'm sorry," Will says. "I don't know." And he puts his head in her shoulder, like a child. She feels the discomfort of her position. Like his mother again. She murmurs, "Shhhh. It's OK."

He is asleep. Dreaming. Will runs down a field, to the water. He can see there is a body lying face down. He grabs the person's coat just below the collar and he pulls them out. But when he has pulled the body out, he knows it is himself.

The next morning, early, Will let Rachel out onto the garden. Drizzle filled every available space, seemingly at the expense of any air. The grass leaked moisture and the path lay drenched by the road which curved around the house. Will stayed inside as she left, not letting his feet pass over the threshold to kiss her, and leaving her to face the thin, wet morning alone.

Rachel pulled her hood up over her head. It flattened her hair and made her look deceptively young. She looked at Will in the doorway, shivering. Neither of them spoke a word about what Will had said in the night. Silence, Rachel thought, that has filled most of her life, can be so powerful.

She'd imagined all this sneaking around was some sort of boyish fun for Will. She thought he was hoping his mum would find out about Rachel staying over this way and then he'd make her see that it didn't matter what she said, what she thought, he'd do what he wanted anyway. That's the way Rachel would have done it. But Will wasn't like Rachel at all.

It isn't a game. Rachel can see that now, staring at him for an extra moment before turning and hurrying down the road. He's terrified. Terrified that his mum will see a hint of truth and try to shut it down before it breeds.

He holds his hand out and lightly touches her arm. "See you later," he says. "I'll come round."

Rachel nods, then walks away down the path towards her house.

*

"Yorkshire!"

"What?" Mary was standing with her wide body shoved against the big sink in the kitchen, rubbing a squat blunt knife over carrots her husband had plucked from his allotment.

"Keith! He's from Yorkshire. And he's coming here today!" Andrea stood with her arms and legs like toppled skittles holding the back door open, breathless.

"What are you talking about, Andrea? Who?"

"Keith. You know, mum, the one I met in Blackpool. You asked me where he was from and I didn't know, but now I do. Yorkshire."

"Yorkshire's a big place," Mary muttered. She laid the scrubbed carrots on a board and began pushing a knife blade down onto them. "And what do you mean, he's coming here?"

"Today. He's coming to see me today. I've just phoned him from the phone box down the road and he says he's setting off right now!"

"Why would he do that?"

There was a pause in Andrea's excitement where she seemed to remember a sour reason, then she said, "Because he can't wait to see me, of course. Oh mum, wait till you meet him. He's perfect."

Mary turned her back and swept the carrots into a pan of water. She could see herself in her daughter, twenty years earlier, and the name of the man she'd fallen in love with bursting out of every inch of her body. And a baby fighting in her stomach.

The doctors told her after the birth she'd been lucky to have that one and she wouldn't have any more. Mary took the news with confusion, and relief. What had just happened to her, bending before her own death in order to deliver another's life, couldn't be called lucky. The luck was in never having to do it again.

She turned and looked at Andrea still in the doorway, her daughter's face like a beautiful harbour that has never known a storm.

"Don't get your hopes up," Mary said. "He might not come. And if he does, just don't get carried away, don't—"

"Mum!"

"I mean, don't go saying he's perfect, Andrea. People aren't perfect. And just remember, he's not from round here. He's not like us at all."

Keith came with a west wind. His train rattled boards on platforms and swept gulls out of its way. It powered through the humped fields. Set the sky alight. Torched the past. Opened the future. And Keith didn't care if he never saw anything else ever again. Only Andrea. What the bloody hell was happening to him? He'd already found no difficulty in dropping his friends, leaving his family behind and quitting all thought of following his father into shop-keeping. Now he let the land go too. It was easier than he'd imagined. He'd heard about women with magical powers of witchcraft, and here was Andrea altering everything he'd always known. She was turning life on its head. It was crazy. But he didn't want to refuse it.

Andrea was waiting for him when the train rocked to a standstill with Keith in the window. They walked from the empty little station, tentatively holding hands. The sky was different up here. It seemed almost as if the tall hills were casting their shadow up to the clouds and everything was as dark as the hills were.

Andrea told Keith it always rains. She smiled. "My dad says, of course it does. We wouldn't have the lakes if it didn't."

And Keith didn't know how he was supposed to react to that. "It rains all the time?" he asked.

Andrea could feel how fragile the beginning of love was. How a simple thing like the weather could alter the course of it.

"Well, not *all* the time," she said.

And he visibly relaxed.

Keith went with Andrea back to the terrace where she lived with her mother and father. Mary was still in the kitchen. Still held tightly to the vegetable knife in her hand as Keith came in, eyeing him as if he was there to swipe his arm over the whole house and clear away their lives.

"Mrs...?" he tried.

There was something between Mary's daughter and this boy that she felt she could reach out her hand and touch. She didn't like it. It made her fingers weak, and her own tongue taste bitter in her mouth just to think about it, but it was there, and it couldn't be taken back now.

"Mary," she said. "You can call me Mary. And thank your lucky stars our Andrea's father isn't here right now."

When Arthur came home, beer so sunk in his body it almost bubbled under his skin, Keith and Andrea were sitting in the kitchen, alone with their thoughts and the lingering flavour of so many strained carrots eaten hours previously.

Keith got to his feet when Arthur pushed the back door and stepped inside. If he wanted the girl, wanted to make an honest woman of her, it was Andrea's father he must convince. Before they could tell Andrea's parents what Andrea had told him on the telephone that day. What Keith had to do was make this man believe that he would have done all this anyway, even without the gun to his head.

The two men shook hands and Arthur turned the other man's name over, under his tongue, deep in his throat. "Murdoch?" he said. "Is that Irish?"

Keith could feel the slender tip of a bargain. Had no idea if it was or not, but he said, "Yes, that's right. Irish."

Andrea got to her feet and pushed her way between the two men. What were they talking about, Irish? What did that have to do with anything?

"Dad," she said. "We've got something to ask you."

She shouted her mother from the bottom of the stairs and Keith grinned uncontrollably, stupidly, while he still held the other man's hand in his grasp and said. "I'd like to ask your permission to marry your daughter, Mr. Barnes."

Arthur shook the man's hand furiously. Felt a connection in their shared roots. Mary rolled her eyes and, glancing quickly and sharply at her daughter's belly, muttered, "God save us, you're not are you, Andrea?"

Then quietly, under her voice, almost addressing the tiny baby she suspects to be there, she whispers, "Not again. Please don't let this happen again."

*

Not the stained glass window. Not the cross. Not the candles or the dried flower arrangements. Something else.

*

Two more weeks have passed since they went to Morecambe, since he cried in the night with Rachel. Gone like forgotten gulls heading for warmer air. Like slipped sentences peeling from lies. And no one else seems to notice how strange the time has been. No one except Will appears to have felt the weight of these stacked days.

He pushes a roller over the earth, squashing and flattening, compacting the mud. Stops. Adjusts the baseball cap on his head. It was too hot for this kind of work. Ironic really. In the winter, when he needs the money and the exercise, he can't get work. But in the summer, when he is energy-less and even too hot to move on some days, everybody wants their garden doing.

He lays out the rolls of turf, unravels them like magic carpets turning over one another. Butts the edges. It's amazing, how it all knits together, grows and becomes one. How does it know to do that? It's like every other living thing. How do cells know what to do? How does life work? How does it stop working once it has started?

He stands back. Rubs dirt on his face while rubbing sweat off. Feels uncomfortable with himself again.

Rachel had been complaining yesterday. Only a few weeks into her pregnancy (how many is it now? – six? – seven?) and she's already complaining about pains. Will wonders what it's going to be like as she gets further along. It can only get worse.

He wonders how he'll cope when she starts being sick, when she gets fat, and then, of course, when she actually has the baby. Not when the baby is a living, wriggling little person, he can't think that far, but when she is actually having the baby. She'll probably want him to be there, won't she? He'll have to... what? Rub her back? Make encouraging noises? Is that what the men do while the women push and grunt?

His dad had tried to offer him some advice yesterday. He tried, in his stunted way, to explain to Will how Rachel would be feeling.

"Women..." he said. "Especially when they're pregnant, they have all these... hormones."

"I know, dad."

"Yes but, I mean, if she... if Rachel seems strange sometimes. If she seems like she's forgotten you, or she just doesn't want you..."

Will had tried to imagine if this could possibly be true of his mum's relationship with his dad. Is this how she acted when Will was born? Is that why she is so distant to him? Did Will come between his mum and dad and break up a love they must surely once have had? Or was it just that she only despised Will?

"Remember, she doesn't mean it, Will," his dad continued. "It does funny things to a woman, you know, having a baby."

Will had seen a dead rat in the middle of the path when he'd parked up at today's garden. It looked like it could still be warm, especially in the cosy, foetal way it was curled up. But its little face looked as if it had been stopped, mid-sneeze, never to finish that one last action.

A rat. A starter of plagues, a carrier of diseases. Will shuddered and then looked up at the clear sky as if he was expecting something. Then he shook himself. Why did he have the stupid thought that this was some kind of sign? He was starting to think like Rachel.

He pulled his baseball cap down so the peak nearly covered his eyes, and tried to concentrate on his work.

He is out of his depth. Knows it. He can feel it covering his head. Rachel, she's old enough for all this. It's biologically right for her, probably overdue really, but for Will it's far too early. Isn't he supposed to have scattered his seed? Isn't that the idea? Like his boss at work says, like Steve pretends he'd done. Like they all wish they'd done. Live a little. Even Will's mum implied that. Like Martin did. Just have fun. Let go. Move from woman to woman with no intentions. Not be caught by one of the first women he sleeps with.

He saw her this morning when she was waiting for the bus. He had often picked her up before. Normally he would drive her to work if he saw her at the bus stop, even if it meant going a bit out of his way, but not today.

Her complaining had worn him down. All the sour words about physical agonies, the aimed implication that he had done this to her. The dragging, she'd said. Dragging pain in the tops of her thighs, the bottom of her belly.

She hadn't looked so good yesterday. Her face was even paler than usual. Will just said it was probably normal. Now, of course, thinking about it, *having* to think about it, he feels bad. What does he know about women's bodies, especially pregnant women's bodies?

She finished work at 6.30. Late, but not unusual. The last two customers wouldn't budge and Rachel had ended up having to squat on the floor with them, picking out books entirely at random and offering them up like notes from her mouth, hoping to find the right one to suit the song.

She touched her back when she stood up again. A wry smile flickered on her face. This is what it would be like, in weeks to come. This is what she would do when her belly was big and her bones were aching with the weight of it: she would forever be holding her back, stretching her limbs, and trying to make herself more comfortable. There would be no sympathy until her belly was bigger with the evidence, even though she was starting to feel it.

She locked up the bookshop, leaning down with her chest close to her hands as she turned the keys in the door. She always did that. Always felt vulnerable when she locked the door at the end of the day. What if some madman came tearing up the street? It had happened at the betting shop not long ago.

The manager was locking the door when two guys grabbed him from behind and forced him back into the shop. Took everything. The poor bloke was well shook up. Said he knew they'd got a knife at his back but he didn't know how big it was until he watched the CCTV footage. Then his nerve endings prickled at the thought of the blade that could have been slicing them in half.

What if an opportunist saw her and tried his luck, wrenched the keys from her hand, forced her back inside, demanded the money from the takings? She couldn't chance it anymore. There was a baby growing inside her. No risks were worth it now.

She slipped the keys into her shoulder bag and walked up Finkle Street. She passed the trendy Italian restaurant, the pub, and the toyshop on the corner. The other shops were all shut now and the pubs and restaurants were taking over their shifts, switching on their lights and their music.

Rachel could smell the Chinese takeaway, where the kitchen staff were already busy frying rice and tossing prawn crackers in a pan. When would the cravings start, she wondered. Would she soon be eating prawn crackers with everything? And would she go off coffee? Better make the most of a good coffee while she still enjoyed it.

She inhaled deeply, more tempted by the hot fried rice than the ice-creams two boys were eating at the end of the little alley that leads to the café. It was doing a good trade, staying open with the evening light, and the beginning of the tourist season.

She probably heard the men running up Finkle Street, but her mind was fixed on the thought of a freshly ground coffee.

If she had seen them she could probably have moved out of their way, taken shelter in the alley while the hurricane blew past her. If she was further along in her pregnancy they would have noticed her bump and maybe, just maybe, they would have been more careful.

The lads were just drunk and didn't mean any harm, jumping onto benches, shouting and pushing each other about, but one of them stumbled right into her, knocking her into one of the boys with the ice-creams, and as she would explain to Will later, they probably wouldn't have noticed if she was in mid-birth there and then.

Can it happen like that? Would it have happened anyway? Rachel thought, for a fooling moment, that she'd wet herself. It's normal for pregnant women to do that, she knew. Although more normal for heavily pregnant women, she guessed. She went down the alley to the café and asked for the toilets.

Rachel had already wiped the ice-cream off her clothes by the time she got into the cubicle, and expected to see the shame of urine-soaked underwear. But she stared down at the inside of her trousers and her knickers which were all mixed together now and entirely red.

She couldn't see where the material changed from one to the other. The blood was down the inside legs of her trousers. She grabbed at some toilet paper and held it to her body. She brought it away again and saw more blood.

It was thick. Fresh like a cymbal. Red like a scream.

She took more toilet paper and mopped up as much of the blood from her clothes as she could, and flushed it all away with her head turned to one side, unable to look. Then she tried to cover herself by using several more layers of tissue in her knickers, and pulled her knickers and her trousers back up. Hurried out of the café. And rushed for a bus with her face as crimson with shame as her blood.

She was just in time for the next one but stood all the way even though most of the seats were empty. She could still feel blood on the backs of her legs and didn't dare check if more was seeping through her clothes yet. If she sat down the blood was bound to show through, so she stood by the doors, with her back against the luggage rack. People were staring at her, wondering why she wasn't sitting down when the bus was half-empty, but she did her best to ignore them, and kept her voice down when she took her phone out of her pocket.

"Will? Can you come round please?"

Will holds the phone loosely, not wanting to hear any of this.

"Why? What's up?"

He can hear an impatient sigh escape her mouth. Like a teacher or something.

"I'm on the bus home now. But can you just come over please? In about half an hour."

"OK."

Will puts his mobile back into his jeans pocket. He leaves his hand there for a moment, holding onto the phone, wondering if he could convince himself that he'd just imagined the terror in Rachel's voice.

When he leaves, the smeared football in the hall makes him think of Martin. Wonders if he would need to speak to him about whatever is troubling Rachel. To talk like other brothers do. But they've never been like that, not really. He moves the football under his toes, backwards and forwards. Then, suddenly, picks his keys up from the little table under the telephone on the wall.

And he walks from the house, bringing the hood of his tracksuit top over his head, feeling the suggestion of rain all around him.

He walks down the hill slowly until he is level with her house. She's there, looking out for him. She sees him and abandons the window, appearing a moment later at the side of the house. Will crosses the road and meets her a few steps from her front door.

"What's the matter?" he asks.

"I've had a bleed."

The first thing in his mind is that he's remembered the rat. *I knew it. I knew it. I knew something awful would happen.* "What?!" he says, unable to believe it, even though it's as if he'd seen it coming.

Will follows Rachel round to the back garden where the guinea pigs used to live. She goes inside and they stand in the kitchen together. His face is still pulled in distortion with horror.

"Today, on the way home from work," she says. "These guys... I think they were drunk, and one of them pushed into me. I thought I'd wet myself, but it wasn't. When I got to the loos it was blood. I think I've ruined a pair of trousers."

He's surprised to feel anger that some man even came near Rachel, but that they did so in an aggressive manner makes him feel weak as well. Bodily weak, sort of drained, helpless. He can't do this. Can't care so much. He knows that to care too much is dangerous. It hurts. He tries to push the feeling away and distance himself.

"It's probably nothing," he says.

Rachel sighs. Is that his answer to everything?

"Don't you think I should go to hospital?" she asks. For once she wishes her mum was there to give her some advice.

Will sits at the big, solid wood kitchen table. He moulds his hand around fruit in a bowl. Pats a stack of unpaid bills. He shrugs. "Do you think you should?" He wants to push the whole idea away. This could be big. He gets the feeling that this could be awful. He wants to go to sleep, to put his head down on his arms now on the table and opt out of the whole situation.

"I don't know," she says.

"Well, it's probably nothing," he says hopefully, trying to be reassuring. "And even if it is... well, then going tonight won't make any difference." He can already feel the problem shifting, moving away with every word he speaks. "So, let's see what you think in the morning. Just go to the doctor's tomorrow and see what they say."

At least he stayed the night. If she had pushed matters too far, he could have walked away, but she was relieved he didn't do that.

Will lay in the darkness and slept with Rachel in his arms. But his dreams were heavy with something gathering speed; something that was inevitable, unstoppable.

In the chapel, on the hill, in the snow. He's gone up the steps, could see the tread from his walking boots, the ones his dad insisted on, forcing snow to crumble. Past the fashioned iron gates. Turned once and looked behind him, but there was nothing to see. Inside, past the organ, past the pews, halfway down, before the pulpit and the Bible on the big stand...

It was coming back this time. He couldn't brace himself against this...

There was a face coming out of the wall. The brass face of a soldier, emerging from the wall like a hand pushing through cloth. And all the names of the soldiers of that village, now dead, being remembered. Those who had been wounded and died.

He opens his eyes suddenly. He's been pulled from sleep. Was that an unconscious act? Did he pull himself out of there, out of the dream?

Rachel is dozing, her head still on his chest, his arm still around her. He knows he can't have been asleep long. He can hear Rachel breathing. Can hear his own heart beating hard. He was dreaming of something he knows he has seen before. It was a memory. Something that's laid buried for years. But what it means, Will still isn't sure.

He brings his arm gently from under Rachel's body and watches her stir and turn in her sleep. He lies still, staring into the darkness; he doesn't want to sleep again, doesn't want to see any more of that memory.

*

She sat still and rigid in the waiting room, staring at the calf muscles of the lady who sat opposite her, perfectly still also. The only time she looked up was when people entered by the heavy glass doors. A woman and her children. A man in a suit, his rectangular briefcase pulling on his arm. And, of course, a heavily pregnant woman. The latter came and sat by Rachel, pushing her cumbersome bump into the air. Rachel managed an ironic smile, skimming her eyes over the taut material around the woman's belly. But she felt she was staring, so she fixed her gaze up at the receptionists, perched on chairs behind a protective screen, flicking their eyes back and forth between computer monitors and patients. The man in the suit stood to one side while they processed and dished out appointments. "Nothing this week," one of them said.

And the man in the suit looked past his briefcase to his feet. Shiny black shoes where his toes wiggled uncomfortably. Aware of how detached the receptionists sounded. He pressed the corners of his mouth together in an awkward smile as he looked up again. The hand of the practice manager was outstretched to meet him.

They shook across the chasm between patients and staff and he was led down the hall. Rachel craned her neck to watch as the two men disappeared behind a door marked 'examination room'.

He was good looking. She thought about him for a moment. Wondered why she still had an eye for other men. What is that? Wasn't she happy with Will?

The receptionist repeated into the telephone, "Not this week, sorry."

And Rachel shifted in her seat. She wasn't ill. But she had got an appointment to see someone straight away. That same receptionist had busied herself checking with doctors this morning, could they squeeze her in? Was this an emergency? She came back to the phone and said brightly, "Come at eleven thirty, the doctor will see you in her lunch time."

Was eleven thirty really lunch time?

Rachel had thanked the woman and imagined the doctor pushing aside her sandwiches and sighing at the interruption. At lunch time, for God's sake. But in the early weeks of pregnancy, Rachel knew she would be seen by someone, somehow. Especially when she had bleeding to report.

As she moved again in her chair, she was still wondering if she would get up to find a shameful red stain underneath her. When she had gone to bed she thought the bleeding had stopped, but there was more overnight, although she was pretty sure Will hadn't even noticed.

The doctor's waiting room was beginning to thin out as the clock ticked slowly past her appointment time and on to a quarter to twelve. She would be going in soon. She practised in her mind what she would say.

It was nearly twelve o'clock when the doctor poked her head around her door and nodded at Rachel. "OK," she said.

The doctor laid her on the strange bed and asked questions

while she felt around the expectant tummy and dribbled gel over it ready for her microphone to expose the voice of a heartbeat.

"So, you think you're pregnant, do you?"

Rachel stared at her. Did she only *think* she was pregnant? Was that the answer? She felt a tickle of relief and a brand new drag of sadness she'd never felt before. "Yes," she said. "I did a test."

"What was the date of your last period?"

Rachel recited the date she had stamped on her brain.

"And this bleed, was it bright red?"

"Yes."

"Anything in it?"

Rachel felt a little sickened by the question.

What was she expecting? A couple of limbs? A flimsy spine? "Like what?" she said.

"Anything. Was it just blood or was there anything else?"

Rachel thought about it for a moment.

"Just blood," she said.

The doctor nodded and moved the implement around on her stomach, searching for a sign of life.

She found none. "I can't find a heartbeat, but it can be difficult at this early stage." She wiped away the cold gel and motioned to Rachel to get dressed. "This happened... when?"

"Last night."

"And has the bleeding stopped now?"

"Yes. I mean... I think so. Well, maybe still a little bit. I'm not sure."

The doctor picked the phone up and put it to her ear and began to dial. She introduced herself down the line and then relayed the story to someone at the other end.

Rachel was still staring at the doctor as she seemed to produce a brown envelope from nowhere and said, "I want you to go straight to the hospital and take this letter with you."

"What? Now?" said Rachel.

"Yes, straight away." And then the doctor smiled like she had only just remembered to do so, like she had realised how important it was. "But you're not to worry," she said.

The first thing Rachel noticed about the gynaecological department of the hospital was how much worry and tension was in the air. How could anybody possibly not worry in here? She was shown to a small room where four other women sat, either staring at the TV hoisted high up in a corner, or flicking through magazines too quickly to take any of it in. They were all worried; about what was going on inside them, about what wasn't going on. She watched one girl opposite her whose boyfriend squeezed her arm and whispered in her ear. Rachel had called Will on the way, but knew he would never make it in time.

She turned sharply as a plump woman in white overalls waddled to the doorway. "Rachel Murdoch," she said.

"Yes?"

"This way."

Rachel followed her, watching the effort it was for her to walk, and the movement of her hip bone beneath her tight uniform, skin, and fat.

"So, this happened last night?" she asked.

Rachel heard her voice break in her throat as she tried to reply. "That's right. I didn't come in straight away because..." she thought about how much she'd wanted to come to the hospital last night and how Will had persuaded her it would be a waste of time. "... I thought it might be nothing," she said.

They reached another room and she was ushered onto a set of weighing scales.

She remembered the way Will had looked hopelessly at her when she had told him about the blood. "How much blood?" he asked.

She shrugged. "A bit. I don't know, how do you measure it like that?"

And Rachel had gazed at the side of his face when he turned away after telling her that going that night wouldn't make any difference anyway. It seemed like several long silent minutes before he sensed her stare and turned back.

"Well? Do you want me to get you to a hospital now? If you want me to, we'll drive out to one now. But I think you'll be OK, just see to it tomorrow. What can anybody do tonight anyway?"

See to it. That's all he wanted. Just see to it. Sort it out.

"You would have had to come back this morning anyway... even if you *had* rushed in last night," the nurse said. "But we get loads of people like that. You know—" and Rachel wondered if it was a hint of disapproval in the nurse's voice "—most mothers are here straight away."

Rachel lay. The doctor was quiet and sympathy was already oozing from his eyes as he moved the scanner over her stomach and gazed at an empty screen. He told her that everything appeared to have come away naturally, but he would give her a pill, just to be on the safe side.

Rachel was alone. She hadn't told her mum yet that she was pregnant and so saw no reason to tell her that she no longer was. Rachel worked for a man who knew less than average about women's bodies and wished he knew even less than that, so he certainly wouldn't want to hear about this. She didn't have friends as such. She knew other women, but always felt as if she didn't fit with them. There was Will's mum, but Rachel knew *she* would be celebrating and not sympathising when she heard about this.

Rachel left the hospital and sat on a bench just outside the entrance. She phoned Will. He answered, breathless, and Rachel could hear the mini cement mixer screeching in the background. He was securing concrete posts into the ground before running fencing panels between each one. So he hadn't even tried to get to the hospital yet.

Even so, Rachel was the one apologising as she began to cry on the phone. She knew how much he hated this kind of thing. Her getting upset. Problems. He couldn't handle them.

"I'm sorry, Will," she said. "The baby's gone."

She felt a tightening inside her. Realised that she had no idea if Will would be upset about this or not.

Maybe he would be feeling it lift from his shoulder right now, the warm swell of relief inside him. That's how she assumed he should feel, how his mum would want him to feel.

"It's all right," she said. She understood if he couldn't come and get her.

Will sighed. He couldn't stand the way he felt. He was caring about it all too much. He said sod the fence, he'd be there as quick as he could.

*

Rachel was born exactly nine months after her mum and dad first met, an incomprehensible anniversary gift, in the brusque, starched maternity ward of the nearest hospital, which, thankfully to Andrea, made for limited visitors as it wasn't that near to her mother's home.

Rachel was born after a quick wedding where the bride smiled through her nausea and the bride's mother kept her eyes on the ground. So even this time, when mothers are supposed to live the day through their daughters, Mary couldn't have the wedding she had dreamed of. Everything, even the polite ritual of speaking and smiling, was strained.

Mary sat in the hospital shushing the baby, her little finger grasped in a tiny fist as tense as a worry. She couldn't help but fall in love with the baby. It's never the baby's fault.

Mary looked across at her exhausted daughter. Couldn't stop herself. "I tried to warn you," she said.

"Mother."

Since the pregnancy, the wedding and now the birth, especially the birth, Mary has become 'mother', said with defeat and hopelessness. Where once she was a mum, needed, trusted and relied upon, now she feels she is suffered.

"Well, I did. I could see what would happen, you know." She shook her head. "Boys of that age always expect..."

Andrea tightened her breath, shifted her body in the hospital bed and dissolved the provocative words in her head, *well you should know.*

Mary looked down at the baby again. It was beginning to cry. The baby's tiny nose was rummaging in its little face, searching for the right feelings, the correct sound.

Mary started to rock from side to side, her body a difficult thing to manoeuvre with the weight and the chair and the child. Above the hurtling noise she said, "Let her know who's boss straight away, Andrea. Don't go spoiling her. And let's just hope and pray, when she's older, she doesn't go the same way me and you have."

Mary peered at Rachel's little face and longed for her to break out of the family pattern. Forced it. "No," she said out loud. "This one will be different. She'll have guts, you'll see. She won't fall for it. Love's not going to trample all over this one."

And then beneath her breath, in Rachel's curled ear, "No, my little sweetheart. No unwanted babies for you." And the words swirled in the air, in Rachel's head, mixed with Mary's emotions and her bitterness, her frustration with her own pallid life, and they formed an instruction to Rachel's little, un-set body.

*

Down by Rachel's feet in the van, an empty water bottle rolled and jumped. Old parking receipts were stuck to the mat. There was loose change balancing by the gear stick. Will had taken off his baseball cap and thrown it into the back. He pushed his hand through his hair. Short and spiky. More so with sweat. Only the bits by his ears, where the hair touched his skin, showed any hint of red staying persistently in each strand.

"You OK?" he asked.

Rachel held herself as if in pain. As if sudden movements could cause further bleeding. As if more of her would fall away.

She nodded. "I'll be fine when I get home, Will."

"I'm not taking you home."

"What?"

"I have to get back to work, Rache. But you shouldn't be alone, I know, and my mum's in. I'll take you to mine and she can look after you."

"You've got to be joking. She hates me—"

"No, she..." Will was struggling with how to change the words. Even *he* wouldn't want to be left with his mum, but he couldn't deal with this. Couldn't be with her right now. Had no idea what to do, what to say. Still, couldn't leave her on her own.

"Will. Come on," Rachel said. "Me and you, it's her worst nightmare. She doesn't want me in the house and she won't be exactly devastated about what's just happened."

He kept looking over at her while he drove. Nothing left in his mouth for him to say. But he knew Rachel couldn't tell what he was thinking. Nobody ever could, not even himself sometimes: it was one of the ways he'd managed to survive so long.

How could he tell her that he just didn't know how this was supposed to go? It isn't something you learn, is it? How was he supposed to know? He drove straight to his house without another word.

"Mum, we're back," he called through the door.

So, he'd already phoned her, Rachel thought.

He stood on the step. He didn't even go in.

"I have to go," he said.

And she suddenly realised that maybe this journey was his way of telling her he was never actually coming back for her again.

Will's mum leans against the sink and fills the kettle. "You drinking tea again now?" she asks.

Rachel knocks the body blow away. "Yes." Looks around her at the kitchen. This weird house. Even on that first night when she was here, it had felt as if the house was adding to the unlikelihood of the situation she was making for herself. Will. A twenty-one year old boy. More than ten years younger than herself. Rachel and Will. What had she been thinking of?

"It might take you a bit of time, you know," Will's mum says. "But you'll get over it. It's not as if it was planned, and you and Will... well, it wasn't serious, was it?"

Wasn't it?

Rachel doesn't reply, lost in a sudden swamp of insecurities. The bond that brought their *relationship* together was now officially lost.

Will's mum makes the tea, puts everything onto a tray and carries it through to the living room, breathing her own thoughts softly to herself. *It's not like losing a real grown-up child. It isn't like that at all.*

She sits down without being asked, and ignores the look in Cath's eyes. She has just lost her baby so she doesn't care about the pleasantries of waiting to be told when she can sit down.

From where she is sitting in this upside-down house she can

just see the back of the field beyond the village, touching the sky. She has to admit it does make the living room more stunning when it is at the top of the house. Much more dramatic than any of the houses down in the village.

These houses up here, of course, are new. Rachel remembers clearly when this land was just land. Just a hill. And then the diggers. And the bricks. And then the people. Will's mum, Rachel thinks, is so typical of those people. She's pouring tea from a stainless steel tea pot, into cups with saucers. Trying to be something she's not. Why isn't she satisfied with who she really is?

"Milk? Sugar?" Cath asks.

"Just milk please," says Rachel.

Will's mum sits back with her tea and looks at Rachel.

"Rachel, there's something I have to tell you," she says. "About Will."

Here we go. "I'm sorry Cath," Rachel says, "but I really don't want to talk about this now—"

Cath is shaking her head. "No, I don't mean about you," she says. "I don't mean that. It's just something about Will."

"What about him?"

"His secrets. He is always keeping secrets."

Rachel thought back to how she felt when it seemed Will was hiding something from her about where he had been brought up. Yes, she had thought at first that he seemed to be keeping a secret. But that wasn't a secret: he simply couldn't remember. So if Will couldn't remember his past, Rachel decided, it was up to her to piece it together for him.

Cath sighed as deep as a mine. "If only I could go back..." she said. "Problems just go with you. There's no escaping who we are, is there? Make him see. It wasn't about where we went, was it?"

"Make who see?"

"Ian. Will's dad."

Years ago. Still like an axe in Cath's head.

"It was him who wanted to come and live here – he was sick of teaching. You know, it's not what it used to be, and he was so stressed. He said he needed to get away. Said he needed to feel the air in his lungs. He'd bought books on the area and had brochures from the estate agents laid out on the kitchen table for weeks. He was serious, I could see that. This was supposed to be the most amazing place, so he kept saying. So I agreed to the idea of a holiday and said we'd think about the rest, the move, you know."

"So where were you before you moved here?"

"York. Why?"

"Nothing. It's just that Will said he was from Manchester."

"Well he was born in Manchester. And he knows that's what is on his birth certificate, but I don't think he can remember anything about York. We don't really talk about it any more. But that's what I'm trying to tell you."

Why can't they trigger his memories by going back to York, Rachel is thinking. If they won't take him there, she will.

"You know that when something terrible happens," Cath was saying. "Your brain, your body or whatever, can't cope with the idea and so your first reaction is to be numb, unbelieving. You know, people wait for someone to come home when they know very well that person is dead. Or they imagine that the person has gone away somewhere and will be back."

Rachel put her tea cup down on the tray. "I'm sorry, what...?"

"I'm trying to tell you about Will. He's got a secret that he won't tell us about."

"What?"

"Well, that's what I'm warning you about. He sort of blots things out. I don't think he can deal with grief.

"You know, Rachel, I wasn't exactly over the moon about you

116

and William. And I can't say I've changed my mind. But William seems to care for you, and he hasn't had many girlfriends... but, well, he'll find it difficult."

"What?"

"You don't understand, Rachel. William is... well, he isn't the most stable person." She seemed to be struggling with her own words, but she said them very definitely. "I am a little worried about how this..." she gestured towards Rachel's body, "will have affected him."

"You mean the baby? Me losing the baby?"

"I'm concerned about him now, Rachel. I thought you should know. What I'm trying to say is, the upset could... you know, tip him over the edge. So I think it would be better if you didn't see him any more. And I mean, really, there isn't any need any more, is there? Of course William will be upset at first, but he'll get over it and in the long run... Rachel. Rachel, are you listening to me?"

Rachel had been staring at the pictures of Will and Martin on the windowsill while Cath's words slipped over her. She realised it looked as if she was ignoring Cath. But she didn't care. She'd heard every word. It didn't make sense. None of this was making any sense to Rachel.

"I think I'll go home now," Rachel said.

"Do you think you should be walking...?"

It sounded like a stunted attempt at compassion.

"I'm fine. Thank you for the tea."

She got up and went out past the lily in the kitchen, with every one of its flowers ripped open at the stalks, and slammed the door.

The drive looks empty with no cars sleeping in it. Rachel looks up. The sky is clear blue for once. That doesn't seem right, the way she is feeling. She walks away, down the hill towards her own house. It makes her angry. Will's mum is fussing over how this may have upset *him*. Will didn't appear too upset to Rachel. As for all that stuff about his secret. That was just weird. She was just trying to put her off him. Didn't Will's own mother understand what it must be like for him?

Across the road Rachel can see the roof of a factory dipped in the valley, and beyond that somewhere is an estuary. She could see it from the living room window of Will's house, from the window where the framed photos are. It reminded her of the day she had stood there when she went to meet Will's family, fingering the edges of the frames and trying to understand how families work. She still didn't get it.

She crosses the busy road, on to the little path that introduces the block of terraced houses. It's all too complicated, too intense. Rachel feels she'll never be any good at this. Is it something that should be instinctive? Are our instincts passed down in the way parents behave? If it was that, then she had no chance.

At least her mum and her gran had not been alone all their lives. But Will had dumped Rachel there at the house with his mother and then ran away back to work. Couldn't wait to leave. Surely he wasn't dumping her for good?

She gets to her back garden and finds the door key in her coat pocket. She's starting to feel a bit faint. She fumbles with the key and the door handle before getting into the house. By the back step, below the hanging basket, empty hutches line up. Full of old sawdust she can't bring herself to throw away.

*

She could do it. She was a mother. A bloody mother. Andrea couldn't believe it. A mother. A wife, for God's sake. But she would do a good job of it all the same.

Rachel was growing so quickly it seemed as if nature had her on some kind of conveyor belt, happily giggling and doing what kids do, towards her wide open future while Andrea's own shaky momentum had broken down and now she was sitting still. What had happened to Andrea's future? Where were the lights she'd seen in Blackpool? And the big wheel, the thrills she and Vivien had dared each other to seek out? Where had her life disappeared to?

Keith had promised Andrea with his eyes that life with him would be amazing. He'd told her with his smile that there was so much more to come. It could only get better. But his eyes and his smile had lied, to get what he wanted that day in Blackpool.

Andrea could see that he was as disappointed as she was with the whole thing. He was destroying himself with his own frustration. Spoiling what little there was left to spoil. But he'd definitely lied, that much was certain.

Andrea was working two jobs now that Rachel was in school: there were bills to pay. On top of that, if Andrea wanted her hair done once a week and clothes from the catalogue now and then, she knew there was no one else around who was going to pay for it. So she worked. One job at the local newspaper, sitting in the typing pool (although it was more of a puddle than a pool) which she did in the week when she felt she should be washing and ironing and picking her only daughter up from school, and one over lunch time on Saturdays in the fish and chip shop.

She had to make her mum and dad believe she appreciated them standing outside the school gates in her place, and she had to tell Keith he was capable of watching Rachel when Mary wasn't free to look after her. *He was the girl's father, after all*, she told him. Even though she felt her words catch on her teeth in her mouth. Who was she kidding? He was as bloody useless as every other bloody man.

So maybe she made it happen. Maybe it was what she wanted, for him to fail so spectacularly. Maybe she couldn't wait for it to happen so she could smile thinly and say *I knew it. I knew you couldn't do this. Can't even look after your own bloody daughter properly.*

Or maybe she was right, and he was bloody useless and he couldn't do anything, and if he was any kind of a man he would have a job, like she did incidentally, and he wouldn't be gambling away what little money they had when he should be looking after his daughter, when *she,* Andrea, was busy making a pittance of money just so he could throw it away.

And maybe then he wouldn't have left Rachel outside the betting shop and the girl wouldn't have wandered off, would she?

Rachel remembers the terrifying adult world he sometimes took her into. Smuggled her into the betting shop because he didn't dare leave her outside alone sitting on the pavement like a beggar girl. But she wouldn't have minded that. It would have been better than going inside. Inside, where the scary, dirty, loud men were all shouting at horses on a TV screen, banging their fists on the wall, throwing screwed up paper into the ignorant air; cursing their luck. And some, stinking of tobacco and lunchtime beer, leered at her bony little body as she passed them, her hand gripping her dad's. Although he never seemed to notice.

Why her mum stayed with him, Rachel would never understand. Once, he must have been like other dads; they must have been a normal family at one time, Rachel thinks. They must have started out that way; they did have family days out, like other people. But even her happiest childhood memory, the day at Morecambe, is weighed down with the knowledge that Rachel's dad ruined it by going off gambling.

If she could only look at him as a man, see him as a person

without his paternal responsibilities, maybe she would forgive his weakness.

Rachel knew her dad came from North Yorkshire. He met Rachel's mum on holiday in Blackpool. Two minutes amid the dodgems and that was it. Love had him. He'd told Rachel this story over and over, a strange twinkle in his eyes, while they walked down into the village together on Saturday mornings when Andrea was at work in the greasy-aired fish and chip shop that made her clothes smell of lard when she came back in the afternoon and her hair feel as if it had been rubbed in salt. Rachel's dad said Cumbria had seemed like fields full of his new love. Hills craggy with life and lakes full of the passion he was feeling every time he looked at his new wife.

But it didn't last, he always told her. His face would fall slightly, as if it was all happening right there in front of them, by the side of the road.

As she looked back on it Rachel managed to catch a glimpse of a person she didn't know in her dad's face. A face she looked back on as someone who'd never expected to find life so hard. A person who couldn't cope. They managed at first, but Rachel's dad had already become gripped by the wild cycle of betting the little money they had – winning, losing, betting more, losing more – and life that was once as awesome as the hills was soon made impossible. What happened to the love? Where had it gone? Does it evaporate like sea water on a rock when the days are too difficult and the nights full of tears?

Rachel had heard her mum crying lots of times. And she knew her dad was never there when she did, because even if he was *there* his will was somewhere else. So where did his love go? Into fruit machines? Did he write it on betting slips now instead of in birthday cards? Did he really think that was love?

Rachel always assumed, had believed, the reason they had moved away was about money: when it came to the point of ruin they decided to move, to get out while they still could. Make a new start, as Rachel heard her mother say. In a city, or at least a town. Somewhere where there were proper shops and better jobs; and nightlife: glittering, sparkling nightlife.

And Rachel hated them so much she couldn't stand to see the backs of their shoes as they walked to the car, dragging their cases, leaving Cumbria for good.

But Rachel can see now, she recognises she had only layered over the truth with the disguise that it was about money. And now the truth was stubbornly poking through. Was that what Will had done, hidden away something from his past? Hidden it even from himself? Was that only the same as what she had done, what everyone does? She'd buried those cold feelings. The guilty sense that her mum and dad leaving was her fault. She had started it.

Could Rachel be blamed at such a young age? Was that why they really left? Because they couldn't stand to see her anymore, this little girl, *their* little girl who had caused them to argue until the sound of each other's voices meant nothing any more. After all, they could have simply split up and gone their separate ways at that point. But they didn't. They left *her*. They left Rachel, not each other.

So Rachel had fooled herself into believing it was about the money. In order to push away the real memory of wandering around the village on her own, while no one even noticed she was missing; while her dad concentrated hard on the TV in the betting shop, willing his horse to come in.

Since he wasn't looking (well, he was never looking when he was in there) she'd wandered back outside, crossed the road, and waited to see how long it was before he came looking for her.

It was her gran who found her, sitting crying on the pavement.

Mary had smiled, but Rachel could see there was something hard stuck behind her eyes, as if she was going to be in trouble. But Rachel was taken back to her gran's house, and given cake to eat. It was when she was taken back home that the trouble started with her mum and dad slamming doors and shouting at each other while Rachel was in bed.

Of course it happened again. It got to the point where Rachel knew she would also get into trouble for running away back to Mary's house, but that didn't stop her.

And as Rachel grew older her mum and dad no longer waited for her to go to bed before they started screaming across the table at home. Until Andrea and Keith never seemed to stop screaming. Until they couldn't stand it. Until they left.

Rachel wonders what they are doing now. Are they silent now or is the air still full of shouts? Would that have happened anyway? But her thoughts are dipped in fear. If she tried to find out, if she phoned, turned up, wrote: the news that was hurled back at her wouldn't be good, she felt sure of that. And Rachel would have to catch the eyes of her own conscience.

They did come back for the funeral of Rachel's granddad, Arthur. They seemed detached from the village then. And their shared, singular life was still intact, if a little frayed. They asked questions. How was she coping? Was there anything they could do? If she needed them... but Rachel's heart was a stone, and she pushed them away.

When they came for her gran's funeral, she was worried that they might decide to move back in. But they didn't want to come and live in the village, or to sell the house. Rachel knew it was because if they did they would have to take responsibility for her again.

And since then, nothing. Just the way Rachel wants it to stay.

Rachel suddenly feels cold. But she realises that she had to hide her true feelings away from herself to get through those teenage years. So what if Will also has a secret? She hasn't told him all about her own past yet.

Rachel touches the dial and the central heating, which she installed after the death of her gran, clicks into place. She walks up the stairs to her bed. Remembers the wood chip that used to be on the stairway and in the bedrooms. Puts her head against a pillow that would have been damp to the touch during the era of the gas fire in the living room, which was oblivious to the needs of the rest of the house.

Rachel's gran used to fill five hot water bottles in winter and lay them in the beds, two in her own and three in Rachel's, fifteen minutes before either of them got in. She used to tuck the pastel striped blankets under the mattresses so tightly you had to get in at the top, onto the pillow and wriggle down. At night, in the sunken bed, Mary used to tell Rachel about her family. She used to weave stories of perfection. Loving families Rachel didn't recognise. People she'd never heard of and wouldn't have felt any connection with except through the way her gran was able to bring them alive.

"My father," she would begin. "He was a proud man. Called my mother queen and each of us his princesses. Wouldn't hear of us girls even thinking about working. Oh yes, very proud. You know, he had his own chair by the fire and if anybody ever sat in it..." and she swiped the air with her flat hand. And she laughed, nostalgic tears welling in her eyes. This was the way a family should be. Close and perfect.

Then, as Rachel got older, Mary began to finger the edges of her own story. She told Rachel that she'd looked into the eyes of her future husband and she'd seen an open sky, a desert road with nothing and nobody else in it. "No signposts," she said, shaking her head. "No clouds. And I knew. You just know, Rachel. When the time comes you will know. When it's the right one. But just remember, your mother and me made the same big mistake. I don't want you doing the same thing. You have to be cautious. You have to hold back. If the boy is the right one, he won't mind that. He'll wait until you're ready."

Mary sat back and folded her arms, satisfied with herself. She'd done the right thing now. She'd told Rachel what someone should have told her, what she should have told Andrea. Hold back. Don't give it away. Don't go giving it up to the first boy who comes along. Don't give away your virginity as if it's nothing. Any boy decent enough would understand that and he would wait.

No, there would be no unwanted babies for Rachel, Mary had seen to that.

But Rachel had stared at her gran in the darkness, light from the houses across the road flitting on her face, excited about a romantic adventure of love, and she'd wondered how to hold her heart back. How was that possible? That was what her gran was trying to tell her, wasn't it? Hold back. Don't give it away too easily. Hold onto your heart. Don't fall in love. Was love a mistake? Is that what her gran was saying? It tied you down. It was all-consuming.

Rachel went with boys, did everything it seemed obvious she was supposed to do, everything all her friends were doing, but she always remembered what her gran told her. And while she gave away her body, she held back with her heart. That was what her gran had said, wasn't it?

And she knew what she had done was a past that Will didn't need to know about yet. But do secrets always come out in the end? Rachel had no idea how Will would react to hers. She couldn't risk telling him and losing him, but at the same time, she felt sure he'd find out one day.

*

Rachel is still lying on her bed looking at the ceiling.

Why do houses seem so important? Rachel has changed the house inside, but it's still the same house. She feels her gran and her granddad moving in the rooms, smells them sometimes, won't go into the room that used to hold their bed for fear of actually *seeing* them.

When she's in Will's house the difference is alarming. The walls are smooth and papered with radiators. The woodwork is everywhere, pale and only lightly varnished. Every cupboard, every surface, every skirting board and window frame is clean, clear, freshly painted and peaceful. New. No ghosts. No memories.

She should hate Will's house. Everybody in the village hates those houses, and the people in them. Half of them are empty most of the year, used at weekends by city workers or as vessels for holiday-makers to dunk in and out of in the summer. They make it impossible for local people to live here. People who just couldn't afford the ridiculous overgrown prices anymore. But she doesn't hate the house. Of course she doesn't. How could she? Will lives in it.

They parked the car by the pub, although as they all got out the kids' faces started crumpling in the cold, their hearts already hardening against this place.

Ian kept going on about how spectacular this lake was. "You can walk all the way around it," he insisted. But Will was fourteen. Cath knew from the way her eldest son, Martin, had been at this age, that fourteen year old boys do not want to walk around lakes in the freezing wind, or do anything else, for that matter, that their parents are doing. She looked doubtfully at her husband.

"Maybe William could stay in the car," she said.

"Absolutely not. We are walking round the lake. Bad enough that Martin isn't walking with us, but Will's not opting out as well."

Cath shrugged, and began walking. She imagined, as she walked, how beautiful this place would be in summer. The track leading down to the lake held her expectant right till the last minute. It had a definite feeling of mystery. As if they were the only ones ever to come here.

When they got to the end of the track, went through the gate and ducked under the branches of the trees, the lake opened up in front of them. It was truly spectacular.

As for Will, his bobble hat was almost covering his eyes, and he peered from under it, with hatred for the world around him; for himself: Cath could see into him. But it was only his age. She told herself, he's a good boy. Always is. Always was. It's just his age that makes him so sullen.

Cath didn't know how long she had stayed sitting there on the sofa. The tray was still on the coffee table in front of her, but her tea was too cold to drink.

She looked at the empty seat where Rachel had been sitting. What did she do? Rachel was gone. Walked out. Did Cath make that happen? She still held onto her cup with the saucer clasped under it. She couldn't say she was sorry if she had. She knew Will liked this woman, of course he liked her, but she was far too old for him. It would never last. And then what? Will couldn't cope with all the upset. Losing the baby had been bad enough, although, of course, that was for the best, but if he got too attached to Rachel, if he became too involved with her, Cath wasn't sure if he'd be able to handle it when it came to an end. And it would come to an end. And then what? Who would Will be expecting to pick up the pieces? Cath was damned if she would be helping him through his silly tears.

When she'd tried again and failed to take a sip of the tea, Cath got up and took the tray back into the little kitchen. She leaned against the sink and looked out of the window. He's been at the lily, she thought. Will had clipped off the leaves and snipped the petals into thin shreds. What was wrong with him? Why did he do things like that? Why did he hate her, want to hurt her all the time?

She wondered, as she always wondered, with growing alarm, if he did it on purpose. Did he mean to destroy things? To destroy life? How do you accept a child who does that? How can you live with yourself when you have brought someone so evil into this world?

Cath crumpled a leaf from the broken lily on the windowsill. You wouldn't think it to look at him. Will always seemed so quiet, so gentle. You wouldn't think he was capable of things like this. She touched the silky petals of the lily, let some pollen fall onto her fingers. It would stain, she knew. Like everything did, but Ian couldn't see that. She could kill her husband sometimes, for bringing them all here.

He'd been having some kind of stupid mid-life crisis, she was sure. Packing up. Chucking his job in and driving to a faraway lake. For what? He had to take a humiliating desk job, pen-pushing for an insurance firm. Cath had been proud of her husband the teacher, now she could barely look at him. If she blamed anyone, she blamed him.

An estuary, far off down in the valley, winked at her as the sun touched it. Cath could see it if she stood and gazed from the living room window. You could smell the sea in the air sometimes. And the lakes, swelling with the rains, leaked onto the roads so that even when driving you couldn't escape the water.

Maybe Will would have been OK if they'd stayed put in York. Surely he would have opened up eventually. They could have got him help. But Ian reasoned that the best thing would be to get away from the house where they were living at the time.

He said Will shouldn't stay there amongst all their memories floating around with the dust. And Cath could sort of understand that. She'd agreed. Hadn't wanted to stay in that house either.

A clean break, Ian had said. A new start.

*

Will worked on the fence as late as he could. Concrete posting always makes this job longer. The digging down to start with. Mixing the cement. He'd told himself so many times that afternoon, he was beginning to believe it.

He'd gone home around six. Parked his van overhanging their drive. His mum was washing up in the kitchen, pots bubbling about under her hands, surfacing on the water and then sinking, like the polystyrene floats Will used to use as a boy in the swimming pool. He waited in the doorway for her to mention the time and to tell him he'd missed tea, but she turned and smiled at him.

"Hello love," she said. "Good day?"

Good day? Will knew there was a reason why he had not had a good day. He knew what it was. But he didn't want to hear about it, let alone talk about it.

"If you want your tea, love, it's in the microwave," Cath said.

Will glanced to his left, pulled the weight of his body away from the door and opened the microwave. He stared at cold shepherd's pie and peas. Shut the door again. From the corner of his eye, Will could see the state the lily was in above the sink. His mum had left it there. She didn't normally leave the dead ones lying around. Maybe she thought of it as some kind of symbol. A symbol of death. A death she was glad about. And then Will realised why she was in such a good mood. He knew she'd never wanted Rachel to have that baby.

Will had to get away from her. He left the food untouched in the microwave and went upstairs. He stood in the shower and watched the water run from his body, until he was ready to hide away in his room.

It's hazy. Difficult to grasp. He's in a familiar place, but his mind shifts from one idea to another and under the cover of the dream he can't pin down where he is. But he knows he is standing by something solid. A person. It definitely has a face and at first he thinks it must be his own face.

He has come upon this image suddenly. Found himself, somehow, standing here looking at it. But it isn't himself Will is seeing. It's made of stone. A sculpture. A pillar of some sort. A statue.

A long gun slung over his shoulder. Boots level with Will's head. A soldier then? Maybe. He tries to look up at the sky, dark with foreboding rain clouds. He can see the darkness of a helmet at the very top of the statue. He still can't see the face. It morphs annoyingly, sometimes it seems to be a feminine face, sometimes hard and masculine.

He lays his cheek against the statue's feet and reaches his arms around the square pillar it stands on. He can feel the cold damp stone on his arms. His hands holding on. He doesn't want to let go. But then he notices there are names etched in the stone. Dead names. The sight of them makes him uncomfortable. For some reason he can feel something building in his body. Anger. An urgency. A scream.

He woke in the early morning. A face in his face. A face he knew, but didn't. He reached out his hand in the darkness. Who was it?

Will turned over in his bed. Turned away. It was like someone was after him. In his head. And he had to get away. But still he couldn't ignore this, no matter how much he tried. And he tried.

Why did they live here? It was a crap place to live. His life was crap here. He thought maybe he'd leave. Yeah, he could just leave.

Get away from his mother, away from Martin, away from this house, away from the water. He'd go back to Manchester. He must have had a life in Manchester. Was sure he'd never wanted to leave Manchester. Can't remember leaving. Why did they leave their home in Manchester?

But the weight of the darkness keeps him pinned in his black hole of a bed. There is a reason he knows he can't leave and go back to Manchester. It has drenched his body. Infected him. He can't leave here, at least not without her.

*

He got up at five o'clock. He dressed in his jeans, his mustard t-shirt, picked up his old leather jacket and then let it fall back onto the bed. Rachel hated that jacket. He smiled. It's the feeling of knowing she is there; he knows that she will always be pleased to see him.

He opened the French doors in his bedroom. Out onto the garden. The sky looked like a million autumn leaves had been blown upwards and were stuck above a thin run of cloud. Orange, red. The colour of watery blood and fruit juice mixed together, he thought. Running into one another. He locked the door behind him and walked down the road. The cold morning was peaceful, uncomplicated. He could see the whole village from the cusp of the hill. The church steeple. The top of the factory to the right, behind the houses. The dull ache of traffic on the road already. As he walked he could see less. The trees began to cover the market square, the pub where he'd had his birthday party, the Spar. Will felt peaceful in the morning, outside like this with no one else around. He felt he could just about stand it out here like this.

When he got there, the blinds were down at Rachel's house. He went round the back, down the alleyway and knocked on the door.

She was in bed. He knocked again, louder this time and heard the movement inside the house, heard a body heavy on the stairs. Rachel unlocked the door and peeked around the edge. She looked at him for a second and then opened the door.

"Will, what are you doing here at this time?"

She wasn't as pleased to see him as he expected. He tried to keep hold of the feeling. "I wanted to see you," he said.

"But it's so early."

She was wearing a white bathrobe that she pulled around her neck. Her hair was nut brown against the white robe, with strands like thick cream where the sun had touched it, bending in the curls. Will stepped inside and closed the door quickly.

"I need to go back to bed, Will," Rachel said.

She walked away, up the narrow, steep stairway, and Will watched her feet, wondering what on earth had happened to the feeling he had woken up with. At the time it felt as if it was the most secure thing in the world.

"OK, I'll come with you," he called after her.

"If you like," she said. "But I'll have to warn you, I've got terrible cramps, so no ideas."

She turned away from him in the bed. She was crying and he realised he was supposed to comfort her. Had no real idea of how he should do that. There were no words he knew that could fill this hole. He reverted back to a time, not long ago, when she had done the same for him in the darkness of the night. Couldn't remember why now, but the sounds she made, soothing and quietening, stayed with him. He put his arm around her and gently sighed.

"Shhh."

This was something Will hadn't done for a long time, comforted someone. He knew he had done it in the past, years ago, and having to do it again now sickened him somehow. It was connected to another time, another person. But he couldn't remember who. He couldn't stand the way this made him feel. Rachel had a point when she'd asked him about people from his past. Maybe that's why he felt like this. Like he was cheating on someone else.

*

In the morning she was alone again. Will had gone. She searched instead for the feel of her gran and granddad, her invisible blanket that had always made her feel safe here. But it wasn't there, when she needed it most. Maybe she was searching too hard. She touched the walls, the tiny things of theirs she kept – trinkets, photos in old tarnished frames, her gran's wedding ring and the port glasses they'd had as an anniversary present – but she couldn't feel her gran or her granddad now, couldn't smell them, couldn't hear their voices, couldn't even remember what they looked like in real life. She stared at the photos again and she thought that wasn't how she remembered them. They were too young in those pictures, before Rachel had learned to stack events and memories in her brain, before Rachel even existed.

She didn't want to get dressed today, didn't want to see a single person, not even Will. He'd left without a word; left her alone with her loss and the anger she felt towards it, and she knew she'd take it out on him if she did see him.

She lay in bed and felt like bringing the covers over her face and staying there, hiding from everyone. Just wanted everyone to leave her alone today. She lay there too long, trying to ignore the clock on the drawers beside the bed, until she had no choice but to phone in sick again. She was sure, if she thought about it, one of the doctors or someone must have told her to do this.

Then she remembered it was a Saturday. She was supposed to

have opened up the shop today. The part-time girl would be there by now, locked out, waiting for her. Rachel had to phone her boss at home. The sound came through in his short, useless words, a low whine humming beneath each syllable.

"Hello?"

"I'm sorry, Tim," Rachel said. "But I won't be able to go into work today. I've..."

She knew he treasured the three Saturdays a month when he could leave the shop to Rachel. But she didn't care if he had to cancel his plans.

"I've... I didn't tell you I was pregnant, did I?"

Silence. She knew she hadn't told him. She hadn't told anybody. Didn't have anyone to tell.

"Well, I was and now I'm not, so I... anyway, I won't be in today. I should be OK for Monday."

"Aaa..."

"I'm sorry I didn't tell you before... I thought I would be able to come in today... to take my mind off things... but I don't think I can manage it, I'm sorry..."

"Oh," he said.

Was that his attempt at sympathy? Rachel realised, too late, that she might have given the impression she'd got rid of her baby.

He sighed. She could hear it. What he said wasn't important, but she could hear clearly every little sound he made.

"OK, Rachel," he said. "See you on Monday."

She put the phone down and the silence was like ice sticking to her skin.

Will had only slept beside Rachel for an hour. Maybe he hadn't slept at all, and then he left the bed, sitting on the side with his back turned for a while, beginning to enter his clothes as quietly as possible.

He managed to get out of Rachel's room without waking her, but when he got home he couldn't get a glass of water without running into his mum.

"Did you stay at Rachel's last night?" she interrogated him.

He looked at his mum as she wiped the worktops in the kitchen with a wet cloth. Was this all she ever did, clean and pry?

But for a moment it was as if there was care in her face; as if something had changed in the way she spoke to him.

"So... you two are still...?" She glanced at him while her hands shoved the cloth into corners and ran it roughly over cupboard doors. "I just wondered, you know, with what happened, whether you would still..."

He felt exhausted. And he couldn't deal with her fake concern. Walked away from the kitchen without a word.

She slapped the cloth down on the drainer by the sink and followed him before he could get to his room.

"William!"

He felt his face become set.

"William. Look at me. Bloody look at me when I'm talking to you."

His eyes glazed. His tongue immobile in his mouth. His teeth tight.

Cath grabbed a framed photo from the window in front of Will. The one of him by the pool, holding up a medal, grinning for the camera, a single click and the moment was kept. Who would believe it? If only all moments could be encased like that.

She shoved it in his face.

"Look at it!" she yelled. "Really look at it. You remember this boy, don't you? You remember this day, being a swimmer, being good at it, really good at it. You remember all that, don't you?"

He just looked at her.

She pushed the photo into his chest and he caught it in his

arms. Didn't mean to. Didn't want to. But what choice did he have?

"I know you remember, Will. I'm not stupid and neither are you. You just refuse to talk to me. Well, I'll get it out of you in the end, you'll see!"

And she left the room. Left Will standing there, with an image of himself in his arms that was different to the one in his head.

It didn't even feel as if he was her son any more.

Then in the evening Martin came in the back door after work. His overalls smelling of sweat and grease, black marks down the front where he'd rubbed his oil-smeared hands. He said he'd left his car at work because the engine was playing up. Talked about it as if it was a child. He said he'd have to beg a lift off Will on Monday so he could get back into Kendal for work.

Cath asked him if he wanted a cup of tea.

"Go on then," he said.

She listened as the water ran inside the kettle. She let Martin sit at the table in his overalls, something she would never let Will do. "It's only a bit of muck from the cars on our Martin," she would tell Will, "not like the clods of earth *you* bring in."

Cath put the mug of tea gently on the table.

"Martin," she said. "I know we don't often talk about... her."

He looked up in alarm.

"But you know, there isn't a day goes by..."

"Mum."

She put her hand on his and felt him pull away.

"Let me finish," she said. "There isn't a single day that I don't think about her and what happened. Well, I don't know what happened, that's the problem."

"What are you going on about?" Martin said. "Oh, I know. You're thinking of talking to Will about it, aren't you? Have you gone bloody crazy? There's no knowing how he will react then!"

Martin drew his hands away from the table altogether and stood up. "It was an accident," he said.

He could feel Cath staring at him. Was it the way he said it?

"It was just an accident," he said again.

He turned in the doorway and watched coldly as the tears began to grow in his mum's eyes.

Half way around the lake Cath turned. Looking back, she will call it a mother's instinct. But if it was that, it was too late. There were no children behind her any more, and it was at least ten minutes since she'd seen any of them. The wind meant she couldn't hear very much, and she was annoyed.

"Ian!" she called ahead of her. "Where are the kids?"

He kept walking. Couldn't hear her either. She ran up to him and hit his arm hard.

"Ian! The kids have gone."

He turned and stared at the empty track. "What do you mean 'gone'? Where have they gone?"

"I don't know, do I? We'd better go back and find them."

They ran back towards the little village, calling their names.

"They'll have gone to the car," Ian said.

But the car stood alone. They checked both pubs and went round the few houses that were there. The last place they tried, in desperation, was the church on the hill. There they found William, asleep in the pews, prayer mat under his head. Cath shook him hard.

*

Will stayed in bed the next day hiding from his memories. Sometimes it was all he could think about, memories building inside him, threatening to take over. He suppressed them when he could. Thought about ringing Rachel or going down to see her, but images and thoughts were circling inside his brain, even though he brought the duvet over his head; and he couldn't make it stop. Couldn't see Rachel like this. Couldn't even talk to her.

He could hear his mum in the kitchen upstairs, cooking a roast as if everything was normal. She would love it if she knew how he was suffering. Even though he didn't want to let her win, he couldn't bring himself to speak to Rachel today.

Rachel waited and waited, unable to stand being alone any more. Couldn't bear the layer of silence that had built on her body since she last saw Will.

He doesn't call. But she's learnt to understand now, that Will won't see that as any kind of barrier. He'll expect the situation, and Rachel, to be fluid.

She got up on Monday and made herself go to work. At least she would encounter people, hear their voices on the phone.

Rachel kept her chin on her chest as she walked from the bus to the bookshop. She didn't walk on Finkle Street and wouldn't even look at it as her feet slid on the cobbles by the pub and the toyshop.

It was strange, but it was easy to look at the pub now. The building used to be the symbol of where her life had gone wrong, but today she could pass it and even stop and sniff the cloud of hops, and it didn't mean anything to her any more. It was the café, and Finkle Street, that she couldn't bear to look at now.

She crossed the road and pushed the door of the shop she worked in. The bell above the door making pain in her head. There's a theory, isn't there, that if you create pain in another part of your body, you forget the original, unbearable pain you had somewhere else.

Rachel stopped in the doorway and let the bell clang in her

head. It didn't work. It could never hurt enough.

Tim was already sitting behind the desk, where he always sat, glasses that looked uncomfortable on his nose, pen in his fingers, magazine on the desk. He looked up.

"All right now, Rachel?" he asked.

Why do men like him, or maybe any men, Rachel thought, manage to make it sound as if they are doing you a favour just by asking that question? As if it takes all their pride, all their dignity, as if they are in some way lowering themselves to ask something like that. He didn't really want an answer anyway, only a simple acknowledgement that he had bothered to ask.

She smiled and made a slight movement with her head. Just enough to affirm, not quite enough to make an answer.

She took her coat off in the back room and hung it up, glanced at the kettle, decided not to switch it on yet. She unpacked the first delivery from the box waiting on the floor by the back door. Dozens of books full of words. What use are words, she thought. Why do people bother soaking up words all the time? They wouldn't make things any better. They wouldn't reverse what had happened. She'd told herself on the way that she wouldn't cry here at work, not in front of Tim. So she had to open the back door wide and step out into the yard.

*

He was stuck. It felt like metal in his head. A twisted, strangled heart. He was stuck between the two. And he shouldn't let Martin influence him one way or the other. Shouldn't trust Martin. He always lied. Will knew that. But he was his brother, his family.

Will had stopped the van before Kendal and stared violently at the windscreen. Then leaned over Martin's lap, sprung the door open and with superhuman strength pushed his brother out.

140

He revved the car away noisily, off to work, but he couldn't get rid of the words, scratching his head violently as if lice had him.

He'd forget it, he told himself, forget that he'd ever heard it. He would simply have to try to blot it out of his memory.

Will parked the van in Kendal towards the end of the morning. He walked to the bookshop, pushed the door with the bell above it, came up quietly behind Rachel. She turned, letting the stacked books in her hands fall.

"What are you doing here?" she said.

"I came..." he stopped, as if he was remembering why he came. "I phoned you at home, but... you weren't in, so I guessed you were back at work... so I... I came to take you for lunch."

Rachel turned back to the books and pushed them into to a standing position.

"Why aren't you at work?" she asked.

"I've finished for today," he said. "I started early and it was only some weeding in an old biddy's garden."

"Oh. Aren't you going to ask me how I am? Since you never bothered to ask me yesterday."

She waited to see if he would deny all knowledge of the miscarriage as well, her crying in the night and the way she'd needed him.

But he just said, "So how *are* you?" as if the words were hardly there and they passed him without him noticing.

He was mumbling slightly. He looked drained. Tired. He did say he'd been up early, but even so, he looked worn out. Rachel watched his face for the secret his mum had warned was in there. But she saw nothing.

"I'm all right thanks," she said. "Though a phone call wouldn't have hurt."

"What?"

"Yesterday. I was home all day on my own and you never called or anything."

She saw him look out of the window and take a deep breath into his body.

"Do you want to go for lunch?" he asked.

She forced a smile at him, but his face remained fixed. She couldn't see his emotions cracking in his eyes. Couldn't see anything.

She looked up at her boss who was sitting behind the counter, busy going through a wholesaler's catalogue, marking down numbers beside titles of books. Will was staring at Rachel. She got the feeling that he was inspecting every pore of her face. She wanted to push him away. The boss didn't look up from the catalogue, but said, "OK, Rachel. Off you go."

They left the bookshop together, the bell loud above their heads in the doorway. They turned on the side of the road and Will began walking up Finkle Street. It seemed to have no significance to him at all.

Rachel was holding Will's arm. She could do this, she told herself. It was only a street, only a place. It didn't *hold* anything of what had happened here. Places, buildings, they can't really hold onto events or people. They can't do that, can they?

Rachel hesitated at the entrance to the archway that led to the secluded café, and Will stopped, oblivious. A sandwich board with the names and colours of ice-creams plastered on it, along with an over-flowing bin, guarded the archway: hopeless sentries which had been on duty that night but hadn't done anything to protect Rachel.

She looked down at the ground and expected to see some evidence of what had happened here. Blood on the floor. A single gulp of breath. Ice-cream from the hands of the two boys and drunken shouts still rattling in the stones by her feet. She tried pushing it all away. Replacing the unwanted thoughts with others, determined to prove to herself that she could go in there. She started thinking about Will's mum, wondering whether she should tell Will how Cath had tried to warn her off again. Would he hate Rachel if she told him the truth? Nobody likes to hear the truth.

She was frowning when they sat down together at a table at the back of the café. They ordered. Slices of pizza and salad. A portion of chips. Pot of tea for two.

"In case you were wondering," Rachel said, "it didn't go too well with your mum the other day."

"Oh?"

"No. Didn't she tell you?"

"No."

The waitress brought the tea and Rachel leaned over the table, her voice a whisper.

"I ended up walking out. She's too protective of you Will. Do you know what she said to me?"

Will didn't answer. He poured the tea and didn't look up.

"She said she's worried about how losing the baby will affect you. She thinks you are... unstable. I mean that's just—"

"These are old pews!" Will said. "Look!" He pointed to the opposite seats, at funny round handles and troughs below them on the wooden ends of the benches. "That's where people put their umbrellas."

Rachel stared at him over the table. "Really?" she said.

"Yeah, wonder where they got these."

She caught a hint of scandal in his voice. Pews in a restaurant.

*

Pews – chapel. Subconsciously he has made a connection. Suddenly, inexplicably, everything seems to line up and bring him back to the same place. That couldn't be a coincidence, could it? It couldn't just be his brain fooling him.

Rachel was talking, cutting into his head.

"Will. Are you listening to me?"

They were outside the café. How did they get outside?

"This is where it happened," Rachel was saying.

"What?"

"Here. Outside. At the end of that alley. That's where those blokes ran into me and I—"

"Oh. Oh yeah." He shook it away. It always worked. No reason why it wouldn't work now. "Did I tell you about the big job I've got on next week?" he said. "I'll be in Carlisle. Carlisle, can you believe that? It's miles away." He forced himself to think about the drive. Alone with the road. The kind motorway that never twists.

"Will. Did you hear me? I said this is the exact spot where I lost the baby. *Our* baby."

She was still watching his face. But she could see he was pretending not to hear her. He wouldn't even look at her.

"Are you all right, Will?" she asked.

Couldn't answer that. She was there. He knew she was there beside him, he could feel her hand, but at the same time, she wasn't anywhere near him.

They were heading to the top of Finkle Street. He knew there was something up here. It was time. Just as if it was printed. An instruction he had to follow. It was the end of all his night diving. All those dreams, those frustrating dreams when he couldn't get to it.

Up to the top of Finkle Street where the main road slices past, where traffic lights annoy the drivers and pedestrians run for their lives. He turned right, looped around a shop and stood facing the buildings where the smell of doughnuts breezed up from the bakery.

And it was there. The statue of the soldier. There were names below it, carved into the stone plinth, curled letters like fingernails scratched on skin.

People who nobody knew any more, still being remembered. These people didn't exist and yet their names were still seen. They weren't alive any more, but the memory of them and what they did, what they meant, still was.

That's how it should be. People shouldn't be forgotten and allowed to just disappear. People should at least be remembered.

People dying, people in war, some who died and some who were dragged away from the battle by heroes who saved them.

A glimpse of the reality of death there in that soldier's face. Cruel death. What if someone had been able to rescue one of the dead men when they were wounded, but hadn't gone back to save them?

I have to do it now.

I cannot fail this time.

Back onto Finkle Street, quickly, suddenly, down the hill towards the river. Pulling Rachel frantically behind him at first, but then letting go of her hand.

She's stopped walking and is standing at the top of Finkle Street.

"Will!" she shouts. "What are you doing?"

He picks up a metal cylinder bin and throws it into the middle of the street. It doesn't slow him down. Just trying to stop the feelings: try to be numb again. It rolls and people move their legs, lean their bodies to get away from it, to get away from him.

What do they think? That he'll kill them? The people are looking at him. But nothing seems to matter any more. Who looks at him. What they think. Even Rachel doesn't matter now.

Especially Rachel doesn't matter now: Martin had tried to make sure of that.

He'd said yesterday that he needed a lift into Kendal this morning because his car was at the garage having its engine poked apart by Martin's boss, and it wouldn't be ready until today. A favour, he said. And he winked at Will, so that Will didn't know if he was telling him about a favour or asking for one. Martin was like that. A constant confusion to Will. Will had told him he'd take him in the van but they'd have to leave the house early.

Rachel.

Martin repeated the name on the journey with tiny blades sticking in each letter, until just before they reached Kendal he'd knocked the blades full-on into Will's head.

She's a slag, why did you ever get involved with her? For a quick shag, yeah, but not to get serious with. You should have come to me earlier, told me who you were having it off with. I'd have put you straight. Everybody in Kendal's had her. For God's sake, Will, even I've had her.

*

He didn't see her at first but Rachel saw Martin there. Will's brother who was watching with a mixture of hatred and amusement as Will started to run amok down the street.

At that moment she realised he was one of the men from the pub she used to lurk in. He had been one of those who had touched her body one night years ago when, once again, she'd drunk too many Bacardis.

But she couldn't remember anything else. Strange that she could have been so intimate with him and yet felt nothing. That isn't really intimacy, she thought. If she'd felt anything for this man, she'd remember his face, his name, the way he spoke. But she'd obviously thrown all that away moments after being with him. Real intimacy, she thought, is more like when you simply can't get any of those things out of your head no matter how much you try.

She'd gone off the rails more than once. Before. A long time ago. Before she really had any idea of what she wanted from life. When she only thought she did.

She wasn't stupid, she knew what she was trying to compensate for, but she didn't know where to find it.

Still, she kept looking. She usually looked for it in the pub. Five years ago, and that was how she reasoned it away. It was five long years ago.

With all the girls from the shops. They always only intended on having one drink. Told each other they would each go home to their quiet houses after that. Sometimes they planned a meal at the Chinese, sometimes even the Italian, but the evening always ended the same way. One drink became another, seamlessly. Their stomachs, hoodwinked by alcohol, stopped asking for food and their bodies, their brains, their blood only asked for more intoxication.

There was always a man on hand to help them with this. Rachel met many men in that pub. Sometimes she was amazed at how many different men would appear. Where did they all come from? She went home with most of them.

Rachel couldn't remember the feel of Martin's hands, the expressions that creased his face or the significance of his body. But now his words were coming back to her. She remembered the words that came from his mouth and the way in which they had sobered her that night.

She knew she had spent nights with many men but she hadn't,

until now, placed any of them in any kind of setting, thought of them as having a family, or a life come to that. The truth was, she'd never really cared about any of them.

Will can see it very clearly now. The face of the soldier coming out of the wall, like the head of a stag in a stately home, maybe the one he always passes on the way back from Kendal, but more real, more alive than that. Will knew the soldier was communicating something to Will, even though his brass face just stared emotionlessly at him.

And Will felt something terrible. He knew something had happened. He knew he should be back outside, stopping something from happening. But he just couldn't do it. He couldn't face the disaster. So he lay down on the pew in the middle of the church. He turned his head away. Maybe, he thought, if he could get to sleep, he'd find it had all been a dream. Maybe nothing had happened all.

He's losing it. Big time. Just like his mum said he would. Just like she'd always told him he would. He wonders if that's the only reason this is happening, because Cath commanded it.

When he could feel his mum staring at him, Will would just shrug, make small talk or ignore her completely. Sometimes there was a tension between them that was so relentless he could understand why people confess under torture to things they haven't done. But he had no idea what he was supposed to be confessing to, so Cath would simply look at him as if she hated him. More than once she had told him he was crazy and that one day he'd totally flip.

So now he shouldn't be giving her the satisfaction. He knows that, but he can't stop. Crying. Screaming. Shouting.

But he could have saved someone. Her. That's what the soldier in the chapel was trying to tell him.

On Finkle Street everybody is staring at him. Rachel is behind him. Doesn't know what to do. She's saying to people, "It's OK, he's all right." She's trying to fend them off. And Will just keeps running.

Could have done something. The only other girl he'd ever loved. The one he's been trying so hard to remember. The one who was gone now. Could have helped her. Could have pulled her out.

And the dream he's been ignoring. The one where he runs down a field. In the dream, at the bottom of the hill there is water. He can see in the water there is a body lying face down. Dead. He feels shock. Devastation. He grabs the person's coat just below the collar and he pulls them out.

He recognises the back of this head, but it isn't until he's pulled the body out that he knows it is himself. In his dream he isn't dead. He gets up again and he's OK.

Just before he gets to the body in the water, he wishes it could be her, and she would get up again, and she'd be OK. But it never is.

He's at the bottom of Finkle Street. He's already left the rational part of his mind behind. What else has he left behind? What, exactly, has he lost? His innocence? His sanity? Or just the capability to ignore anything that cuts him? He felt things falling from him as he walked on. Slipping away. Old memories. False ones. He reaches the end of the pedestrian area, passes the bookshop. Keeps going. Rachel is still trying to catch up, telling the people gathered by the side of the road that there's nothing to worry about. Will can hear her, but he keeps going.

He comes to the bridge. Sees the river. Just like the dream, water at the bottom of the hill. And it all makes sense. He goes over the bridge where the water moves like eyes along a page. Scrambles down the bank. He can still hear Rachel from back over the bridge, shouting at him now. His name out in the air, the sound of it wafting in the wings of birds.

She's left the people behind her, disregarded them, and is running over the hump of the bridge to get to Will, shouting.

"Will! Wait! Stop!" Each word is a shock in the cold air, but he doesn't stop.

He slips on the stony ground by the river, his trainers skidding on the mud. Into the water his legs slide on the bank like the smooth belly of a boat, with hardly a splash. The backs of his trousers are wet now. His feet in the water. His ankles. Then his calves. It's cold, but his brain won't let the information in, or it mixes it and punishes him with it. He should be cold. He deserves it.

Then she's there, someone he's known along, she's there in front of him like a tree he can touch, a song he can hear. Something he's waited so long for and ignored and needed: he's in the water with her.

She's drowning all over again and this is Will's second chance to save her. It's obvious. Blindingly obvious. Everybody deserves a second chance, don't they, to put right something that was wrong. This time he is here. Not hiding anymore. Not pushing the world and reality away anymore. Not scared and sleeping in the chapel.

His movements are slow in the water. But he can't touch her: she isn't floating on the surface like the body in the dream. He grabs, but she's under the water like a ghost in a painting.

Outside the chapel, on the road, getting into cars, Will saw his mum's face staring at him. Why hadn't he done something? What was he doing? If anybody could have saved her, Will could. He remembers his mum's hands slapping him, knuckles bent, hitting him, with a face gnarled like she was spitting. The policeman pulling her away and Will, a hand on his head, being manoeuvred into a car. Then nothing.

Will's dad got up the next day and it was as if nothing had ever happened, but everything about his mum had changed: she had once treated Will like most mothers treat their sons and now she hardly acknowledged him at all.

He's in the water. He can see blood that he knows shouldn't be there.

So much blood. But people who drown don't bleed. Maybe that was a blessing. He's not sure.

The blood of his baby dying and being rejected by its mother's body. An alien thing now. Not quite a baby, but still, not quite nothing. He rejected it, didn't he? Maybe, he thinks, somehow, that's why the baby died.

If he'd been there... if he'd been there, not hiding in the chapel, not being selfish, not ignoring Rachel when it suited him...

Not a baby. Not a baby. And perhaps that's his fault as well. Perhaps everything is his fault, just like his mum's face, silent and still, says it is. The blood from Rachel's body.

He wonders how long it takes to drown. The water is silencing his breath, filling up his lungs and expanding his flesh like a sponge.

It would be fitting, to die like this. It would atone. Maybe *they* would all be sorry when he's dead, and maybe his mum would be satisfied then.

But he can feel something on his head, pulling his hair. He can feel his shoulders, being lifted like a heavy load. Suddenly he's out and he drinks cold air. Somebody is laying him on the riverbank, rolling his body onto its side, coating his clothes in mud. He's being squashed, but he can't tell where the weight is coming from. It feels like his body is being crushed. And water is coming out. He can see it, hear it, feel it, coming from his mouth. Rachel is kneeling on the ground beside him.

"Theresa," Will says. "She's in the water." He steals a glance back at where he was in the river and he sees the empty water travelling slowly over rocks under the bridge. "I saw her," he says. "I have to help her!"

"What are you talking about?" Rachel yells. "There's no one in there!"

"No, I can help her! She's still in the water. I have to save Theresa!"

Once he could stand he was walking away. People tried to hold him back. They said he should wait for the ambulance, but Will had to get away. He stumbled up onto the road, his clothes cold and heavy on his body, his feet rubbing against the cruelty of his wet socks and shoes.

He held onto the wall of the bridge for a moment and looked over at the current below. There was life behind him, in the cars and the people on the street, but down in the water there was only death. He thought about it: leaning over and falling back into the river. For a moment it seemed right. But Rachel was running up the road, calling his name and he had to get away from her.

He carried on, past the bookshop where Rachel worked, the posh Italian restaurant, the toyshop on the corner, and on to Finkle Street.

Here is the alley leading to the café. Here they sat only half an hour ago. He wanted... what did he want? He had wanted to make her feel better but it was all going wrong. Was that what he really wanted?

Here is the place Rachel lost her baby. OK, *their* baby. If she says so, their baby. He didn't know any more. Not now he'd listened to Martin.

Here some drunken idiot barged into her and sent her insides into shock, told the foetus it couldn't possibly stay in such an unstable body, sent it into the world, killed it, rejected it, rescued it... saved it from him.

After all, what kind of a father would Will make anyway? Ridiculous. He didn't have a clue. Could hardly take care of himself, never mind a child.

He's standing outside the café, leaning on the entrance to the alley. Shivering and dripping river water onto the cobbles. But there are people running up Finkle Street behind him. Shouting. He can hear his name, although he's straining to hear it being called. There is another sound drowning everything else out like a bell in a tower, covering the walls of his thoughts, every whispered word inside him. It is too loud in his own body. How can anybody make this stop now it has begun?

She is dead.

And Will is still screaming.

*

"We have to go, Rachel. You know we can't stay here."

Everybody had gone. They'd buried her gran, the neighbours had slid back to their own homes, and her mum and dad couldn't wait to get away.

Andrea was already in the car, fussing with the directions again, checking her make-up in the mirror and smoothing her skirt against her knees.

Rachel was happy to see them leave. This was her home. Not some city she'd never seen and felt no pull towards. She was looking forward to the independence of having the house to herself.

Not like the time they left her the first time, when she didn't want them to abandon her.

Back then Keith had thrown the bag onto the back seat as he slid into the car and Mary's hand patted Rachel's shoulder as the engine began. Rachel saw her dad's eyes, full of hopelessness and loss, trail in the air. And her mum, rubbing her hands in the cold, pulling her coat tighter around her chest, and waiting excitedly like a child for the biggest surprise and adventure of her life.

So Rachel had moved into the spare room in the old terrace house at the bottom of the hill. She ate her gran's liver and onions and home-baked scones, watching all the time how it was done, how these things were made. Maybe, she told herself, one day she would claw back some kind of normal family life and this knowledge would come in useful. She filled her head with how to make, how to do, how to grow, and these busy things meant she wouldn't have to think about what was now missing. And she thought herself extremely lucky. It could be worse – for some people life was a lot worse. She read about it all the time in the papers, misery, robbery, accidents, kids going missing, even murder.

One day when her gran had made a pot of tea in the black-stained silver teapot, her granddad, ever matter of fact, sat at the kitchen table reading the local paper. He threw it down on the table between the cups and the sugar bowl when he'd finished reading it.

"Aye," he said. "Terrible business."

At first Rachel thought he was talking about what had just happened, her parents abandoning her without a second thought, and she felt her senses prickle. Her granddad never talked about things that actually happened. *Things* happened to other people. She stared at him until he felt her gaze burn his old cheek and he looked up.

"I said, terrible business." He hit the newspaper on the table, flicking it slightly with his yellowed fingers. "Girl gone missing in the hills," he said. "Shocking it is. Aye, she'll be dead."

Mary turned sharply from the sink where she was soaking old cloths in bleach. "Arthur!" she hissed.

"Well, stands to reason. What else can have happened to her? Body will turn up, you'll see."

Rachel felt the dreary rain begin to hit the windows and thought about how bad it would be to be missing out in the cold somewhere and everybody thinking you're dead.

It was a memory that pricked her to tears on the day of her gran's funeral.

Everyone had come back to the house, Rachel's house, for tea and cakes after the service at the crematorium, and when her mum and dad had left she had to clear up after everyone. She went to the fridge and realised someone had used up the last of the milk. She left the house, feeling slightly relieved the day was almost over, and headed down to the Spar.

She picked up the milk and then hesitated at the counter, eyeing the local newspaper.

"Bad business, that," the man behind the counter said. "Kid gone missing up in Buttermere, little girl. They say she was on holiday with her family."

Rachel picked up the paper and laid it down in front of her with the milk.

"Worst thing about it is," he continued, "looks like the lad had something to do with it. Well, I say that, you know, police don't know as much, but it's a bit strange, don't you think, for the mother to be blaming him. What kind of mother blames her own son if she doesn't know it's true? Something in that, I'd say. And the lad, only fourteen he is, won't say a bloody word. How's that for a guilty conscience, won't say a bloody word."

"Barry!" scolded his wife, appearing from the stock room, hissing just like Rachel's gran had done to her granddad. "Shush now with all this. Rachel doesn't want to hear anything so morbid, specially not today."

She did not realise it was she herself who made Rachel cry with the memory. Nor that Rachel stayed awake all night thinking about the girl, hiding in a bush because of an argument, or wandering over the fields, oblivious to the time, or much worse, and it seemed much more likely, snagged on weeds at the bottom of the lake. And the brother, devastated, unable to speak for grief and shock, and everybody taking it as a sign of his guilt.

*

When the police came and stopped their cars at the top of Finkle Street, hands holding the dull thud of weapons in their belts, Will had looked at them with pure terror, and struggled wildly.

"No, leave him alone!" Rachel shouted, wondering in the back of her mind if he had actually done something terribly wrong, something she didn't know about.

But a large policeman stood holding her back and said to Will, "Come on now, lad, that's enough. You're upsetting the girl."

Rachel realised her face was wet with crying and she must have appeared hysterical herself. What a pair. It seemed almost funny for a moment.

The police had him in the end. But not in suspicion. They took him to the hospital where doctors dried and warmed his cold, clammy body, peeled the sodden clothes away and wrapped him in a gown and a blanket. Then they checked him for drink and drugs and asked him a series of seemingly random questions.

Then made him stay in overnight.

Rachel was there when his dad came, and they talked while Will slept under the effects of the pills the doctor had given him.

*

Rachel was still there when he woke up in hospital in the middle of the night.

"Theresa is dead, Will."

He needed to hear the words. Had never heard them before. Rachel repeats it. Callously, coldly, unflinchingly she says it again.

Theresa is dead. Yes, he knew it. Behind his eyes, his ears, his heart, in the centre of himself he knew she was dead, the only girl he had loved before. But he'd never actually heard it. Since that day she died, he hadn't heard her name mentioned at all.

She'd never existed in the first place. How can someone die if they've never lived? How can you accept a death if you won't acknowledge a life?

"Theresa is dead, Will, but it wasn't your fault."

Not my fault? How do you know that? Everyone says it was.

Did he stand by her grave? Can he remember that? He thinks he did. *He thinks he watched her being lowered into the ground and thought about her. He thinks he will remember more now. The way the coffin was lowered into the hole like a pallet of bricks on a building site. The look on his mum's face. Useless flowers and cups of tea after. Stifled grief. Stunted love. And Theresa. Bloated with water. Dead. He let all the thoughts roam through his mind, couldn't stop them. Thoughts are like rocks. Like rain.*

Will has no idea how she was found. Was it that same day? He knows he was wrapped in a blanket. The police came and everybody seemed to be waiting for him to tell them something. *Where is she William? What happened?* Why couldn't he speak? He had nothing to say. He knew anything would have been better than nothing at that moment. But his face, his throat, his eyes, his ears felt as if they had given up and would never move again. *Where is she?*

Will's mum was hysterical outside in the snow. Maybe that was why the policeman looked as if it was all too much for him. Cath was shouting at people to hurry up and find her baby.

When was she found?

Why does nobody talk about it? He's been allowed to forget. Do they all feel sorry for him? Think he can't cope? Or do they hate him so much they can't bring themselves to be honest with him? Does he deserve that?

He'd taken her to the back of the house and played basketball with her for ten minutes while their mum and dad went around the house checking windows and pulling plugs from their sockets. They eventually got into the car, still playing together in a game of rock-paper-scissors.

Their mum leaned from the front seat and said, "Thanks Will," because he had entertained her and prevented her from becoming impatient. But he didn't need the thanks. Couldn't understand really why his mum was even speaking it. Never needed it. She was his sister.

They listened to his dad, going on and on about this amazing place he'd found. Somewhere away from it all; wild, or so their dad had heard, where he wanted to take them, to feel the freedom of the open air. He expected them to gather it into their hearts and bodies in the same way he had.

"When we live there..." he'd said. And Will and his sister exchanged worried glances on the back seat of the car.

Theresa giggled on the journey as Will muttered about how far it was to the countryside. With the motorway in front of them, flat as a single breath, straight as an outstretched arm, seeming to go on forever.

159

At first there was candy floss, sticky on her kissed lips, but it wasn't too long before life wickedly, unfairly, pulled Andrea's feet from underneath her and cruelly held them to the ground. Told her body it must obey. This is the way of life. This is how it goes. These are the rules.

Andrea had to admit to the small swelling in her stomach, and she had to get married; everybody said so, her mum, her dad, and even Keith.

But Andrea's own heart still struggled to accept. This wasn't the way it was supposed to be. It couldn't be. She couldn't live a life like her mother had done. It just couldn't be like that. How could it be? What had Mary ever known of love, passion, sex? It wasn't the same. Not like Andrea and Keith. It couldn't ever have been like that for Mary, could it? And if it had, how could she have been satisfied with all the years of nothing that came after?

Andrea said her generation of people were different. She said they didn't have to live by the same rules. But she looked into her mother's eyes and saw through them, how she was laughing.

*

The day after Will has been let out of hospital Rachel locks the back door behind her. Nervous about where she has to go today. She has phoned in sick again. Leans over the Perspex by the steps where the guinea pigs used to be. Walks through the alleyway and out onto the road.

The path evaporates after Rachel's house and she has to cross over or walk on the road itself. She crosses. Runs before more lorries power on.

In the car, driving to Buttermere, Will saw Martin slumped against the window, walkman on, the high fizz of the music seeping from his headphones.

He knew Martin was eyeing him with Theresa. They were a handshake. An unspoken rule. A silent dream. Theresa never giggled with Martin – and Martin never played games all morning with Theresa.

But Martin's air of disapproval overpowered Will and made him feel out of place. He was fourteen now. Should stop such childish games. But then Theresa had looked at him with needy eyes and he'd given in and suggested spotting cars and I-spy, while Theresa waved at lorry drivers.

"I tell you kids," their dad said from the front seat, turning slightly towards them, "you'll never want to live in a city again."

Will just rolled his eyes at his sister as soon as his dad was concentrating on the road again. Theresa giggled, falling dramatically against Will's shoulder. And Martin turned, music in his head, with a look as black as the bottom of the sea and muttered, "Stupid, you children, just stupid."

Up the hill, and round the winding road to the house at the top. No.1. Will's van still overhangs the drive. She ticks off the cars. His dad's car is missing, but Martin's is there. She knocks on the door and hears footsteps. A key being turned in a cold lock. The door opening. Martin standing there.

Martin was so full of hate. Tried to close the door in her face.

"He isn't here anyway," Martin said.

He was probably lying, Rachel thought. Although it could be true. Will could have left his van behind.

"It doesn't matter," Rachel said. "It's you I want to talk to."

"Me? Oh, so you've come to ask me why I told him."

She looked blank. "Told him what?"

Martin opened the door properly again and smiled at her. "You don't know?" he asked.

She shook her head.

"But I thought that was why he went..."

"What are you talking about, Martin?"

He stood back and Rachel went into the house. Martin had no shirt on and Rachel found it impossible to believe that she'd ever known this man in any way. She looked at his chest and she wondered what it had felt like when she'd touched it. His feet were bare, his jeans hanging beneath them so that he trod on them with every step he took. She should know those feet, Rachel thought. How could she not recognise those feet when they'd rubbed against her shins in the night and lain tangled with her own toes while he'd dozed?

She closed the door and followed him into the living room. He flung himself down on to the sofa and continued smiling at her.

"So Will never said yesterday why he was so angry with you?"

"He wasn't angry with me," Rachel said. "He just went mad. Your mum told me she was worried about how well he would be able to handle... it."

"That's all it was, was it?" he mocked.

"What do you mean...?"

He sat up quickly and leaned forward. "It could have been more to do with the fact that I told him what you're really like."

There was a feeling inside Rachel like a sudden blast of alcohol. She could hear her own heart.

"You didn't think he'd never find out, did you?" Martin said. "He's my baby brother. I'm looking out for him. I don't want to see him with some slag who's had half of Kendal. Especially not when she tries to trap him with a bloody baby."

"I didn't trap him! How can you say that?" Rachel had an urge to hold her stomach, to protect an invisible being again.

"That's what it looked like to me," Martin said. "Anyway, besides that, don't you think he had a right to know that you've already shagged his brother? He had to find out sometime. And come on, Rachel, be honest, you only wanted Will to father a baby because you know you haven't got much time left. Those eggs aren't what they used to be, are they? I can't think why you didn't just go back to the pub and start picking up blokes like you used to. One of them would have been desperate enough to oblige you, I'm sure."

Downstairs lying on the bed. Hands behind his head. Despite pulling a pillow around his ears, he could still hear every word. Will had woken up from his drug-induced sleep to the sound of their voices.

It took him a few moments to realise he wasn't still in the dream. Martin's voice slipped easily from one to the other. But in Will's dream his brother's angry voice was only a whisper. Not powerful like it is now. Not arrogant. Not strong like the rocks tumbling down the hills.

Will got up off the bed. He hadn't done that yet today, hadn't eaten or cleaned his teeth or done anything yet today. He pulled a pair of jeans from the chair in the corner of his room and threaded his feet through the legs. Opened a drawer and unrolled a pair of socks.

Outside, the rain was splashing on the path and disappearing into the grass. But drops were still surviving on the French doors and the windows, holding on as they trickled down the panes. Will went upstairs quietly, his feet, warm in socks, undetectable on the carpet. He could still hear Martin going on, his words aching with poison, and Rachel silent, unable to defend herself against this. Well, how could she? She knew it was true. But still Will couldn't stand it.

Will went to the little kitchen, opened the cutlery drawer, and looked inside. A bread knife. He thought about the man in his garden stupidly trying to prune a tree with a bread knife. Too blunt. Bread knife is too blunt. He closed the drawer and ran his fingers over the other blades in his mum's knife block.

"What did you want to talk to *me* for, anyway?" Martin said.

"I want to know what happened to Theresa."

"Theresa!" Martin spat the name under his breath.

"I know your mum won't talk to me, especially not now, but you're his brother, you must know what's going on. So what happened to her?"

"Will killed her."

"*Will* did?! No, that's impossible!"

"No, I'm telling you what happened! Will killed her, his precious little sister. He had the chance to save her in the lake, but he didn't. So as far as I'm concerned, and as far as my mum's concerned, Will killed her, even though the inquest didn't say so exactly. That's all there is to it. And that's why he's been such a bloody basket case ever since."

Rachel fell backwards into a chair that reached out its upholstered arms to catch her.

Martin laughed. He moved his head slowly from side to side. "You thought he was the gentle type as well, didn't you!" he said. "Let me tell you something about my brother, the killer, and his victim. They were like Siamese bloody twins when we were kids. Always the two of them. Inseparable. And never paid me a scrap of attention. Never bothered with me. No, it was all about Theresa with Will. Anything to please Theresa. And mum and dad loved that, you know. Always going on about how good Will was with Theresa, how great it was that they got on so well... but it turns out Will wasn't as close to Theresa as they thought."

He shrugged. "But he couldn't remember any of it afterwards, from the shock. And now we've even had to hide away all our memories of her because no one knows what he'll do when he remembers what happened," Martin sneered. "Sounds to me like he finally remembered in the river..."

"And that's your idea of sympathy is it?"

"Don't talk to me about sympathy. Look what you've done to him! You know, I think he actually believed in you and trusted you. And then he found out what you're really like. Are you happy now? You've torn him apart."

"*I* haven't done anything. You didn't have to tell him."

Martin and Rachel both turned to the door. Will was standing there.

"Yeah, he did, Rache." he said. A blade was motionless in his hand, down by his leg. It seemed more dangerous with his chest bare; so much clean, unmarked flesh.

Rachel stared at him. "Will, I thought you were out," she said.

"I know you did. I heard *him* tell you I was. I heard everything both of you said."

"Will, I..."

"Don't try and explain, Rachel. You can't explain this."

From the sofa, Martin slowly stood up and moved forward, towards Will.

"Like I told you, mate," he said. "She's not worth it. She's just a slag."

The words were like too much unstoppable water, covering Will's head, in his eyes, his ears, his mouth, rushing in his brain. He had to shut him up. Martin was doing it again, trying to ruin everything, trying to take away the one person Will cared about.

Will moved, one swift action, and Rachel thought he looked as beautiful, as graceful, as he does when he pulls his t-shirt over his head to undress. Or when he slips from his van in the rain, rushing to get in the house. One quick movement. Blade up, going at Martin, but in the end it was quicker than Rachel could understand. She could see his face, seemingly without any feelings, unattached to the emotional parts of his body. Just blank.

His eyes slightly widened and his mouth set tightly in concentration. Or was it the only spark of anger she would ever see in him? He held his hand high over his head. The knife like a splinter of ice. And he brought it down on his brother.

The knife, done, had bumped on the floor, thrown away, blade shuddering. Blood was dumped into the carpet. Rachel had been quick, snatching cloths in the kitchen and then crouching by Martin and tying them around his wounds. In his shoulder, awkward to get at. In the thick muscle of his upper arm. Made sure he didn't lose too much blood. But she saw him on the ground now, scared, pathetic. And she thought about how he had lain with her one night after the pub, years ago, telling his story, so shockingly relevant now, about the body in the lake. And how Martin had left Rachel lying there with his story of death still in her head, in her broken dream that morning.

How he was the one who sealed it: who scared her and opened her eyes, made her stop her destructive life. The last one before Will. And she hadn't let herself think about that, their brotherhood. The same blood when they were cut.

She looked up from her position on the floor. "What were you thinking of, Will?" she said. "What were you trying to do?"

"Is it true?" he said. "You and Martin?"

"There was no 'me and Martin', it was just—"

"Just a shag, yeah, that's what he said." Will looked at his brother, saw the terror in his eyes as his life was sighing from his body. And he looked at Rachel, checked her face for a sign that she had any love for Martin, any compassion. He could feel his useless jealousy eating him. Did she care?

"It was a long time ago, Will," she said. She tied knots tightly at the side of Martin's arm.

"I suppose you think that makes it OK," Will said. *It was a long time ago.* I don't have that kind of a past, Rachel. I don't have any kind of past. Have you any idea what it's like to remember nothing? Or to be so scared of the little bits that you do remember you just..." he made a movement with his hands, shoving the air, "... push them away?"

Then he let his body sag where he stood, filled with years of his mum's anger, his own lies, and the confusion that weighed him down. "I can't deal with the thought of you being this other person, doing things. I can't deal with any of this."

"Will, you must have known—"

"No. I didn't know you used to sleep around. For all I know maybe you still do."

Rachel got to her feet. There was a smear of blood on her hand. Will stood looking at her, wiping her hand with her other hand, passing the blood from one to the other.

"Do you?" he said.

"Will."

"Well, do you? Was that baby mine, because I'm starting to wonder."

Will would think, afterwards, that the way they ignored Martin felt normal. Martin didn't seem to be feeling any pain at all. He was so quiet, so full of fear. But then Will noticed him moving his other, un-mutilated arm, stretching it out to reach for the knife, and Will bent to pick the knife up, quickly, too easily, before Martin had any chance of touching it. And then the pain, that Will could not fail to notice, shooting in Martin's body every time he tried to move.

Rachel stared at his wounded shoulder for a moment,

167

examining the taut wet cloth she had applied as a bandage, red as an open belly; noticing the shadows in his upper arm caused by the light from behind him. And Will looked at her, watched her watching Martin, and looking at the knife in Will's hand.

"Well?" he said. "Tell me."

"The baby was yours, Will," Rachel said. "I don't sleep around any more, not for ages, not since I've been with you. I only did it before because..." she shrugged. "I was... looking for something."

"What?"

"I don't know. I was looking for love. I wanted to be loved, I suppose. I wanted the love that I never had as a child."

"What do *you* know about that?" he muttered. "How can you possibly understand how it feels to be unloved?"

"My parents left me," she said. "I've never talked about it, but they just left me here. They didn't want me, not really. Nobody ever did, except my gran and granddad and then they died. I needed... something, Will. I know I should have told you. As soon as I realised it was Martin... but I didn't recognise him at first. I'm sorry. I was sacred."

"Of what?"

"Of losing you. That would be... I was scared you'd leave me too, like everybody else did."

Will reached forward and touched her fingers. Martin's blood was drying in lines on the palm of her hand. Her life line. Love line. Dyed into little red rivers.

*

Will was still looking at her as he walked into the kitchen with the knife in his hand. He reached over to the sink and tossed it into a bowl.

What had happened inside him? Rachel followed. She tried to

see it in his face. What was going on in there?

Will was breathless. His shoulders rose and sank again, a new reality beginning in his brain.

"What shall we do?" he asked her.

"I don't know, call an ambulance? How badly do you think he's hurt?"

Will shook his head. "No. Not that. I didn't mean that."

"What?" she said. "What are you talking about then? What are we going to do about what?" She paused and stared at him, thinking about Martin still lying on the floor in the other room, his blood still draining away. She could feel the time passing. Like she could touch each second if she tried.

"We've got to get out of here!" he said.

*

"Will! Wake up! Where's Theresa?"

He looked dazed. But Cath could already see the panic and terror moving under his skin.

"Where is she?"

"She's not with me," he said. There were tears in his eyes and in his throat. Grief beginning. But he said he knew nothing about what had happened to her.

The police car tagged the ambulance all the way to the village. The older of the two officers grew more and more uneasy as they approached, his busy eyes fanning the frozen lakes as they drove. Imagining little lungs full to bursting with dirty water, listening for the sound of a gurgling throat caught in a grip of ice and drowning in desperation. They knew all along that this girl wasn't going to be found alive.

"Gets to you, you know, when you've got your own," he said.

169

"What do you mean 'we've got to get out of here'?"

"I mean... we should leave. We should go now."

"What? Where? What about Martin?"

"To the lake. Where it happened."

"Buttermere..." Rachel thought aloud.

"Yes, that was it! Buttermere. We should go to Buttermere. Right now. Don't know why I haven't done it before. I never got a chance to say goodbye to her. Nobody ever let me get over it."

"What about Martin?"

"Will you stop talking about him? Just stop saying his name."

Will pulled his tracksuit top down from a hook by the front door. Put it on. Zipped it up. Left the hood hanging behind his head. He slipped his feet into his trainers, got the knife from the bowl in the kitchen and took Rachel's hand. Pulled her through the door. Slammed it shut.

"Will, where are your mum and dad?" she asked. "When will they be back?"

She was thinking all the time about the minutes, the hours. Time seemed like such a ridiculous notion now.

He shrugged. Unlocked his van and opened the passenger door for Rachel to get in.

"But where are they?" she asked again.

His mum had all the ammunition she needed now. Will knew it. A full artillery of his behaviour to use against him. Losing it on Finkle Street. Frightening people with his screaming and shouting. His ridiculous behaviour in the river. Abandoning his bleeding brother. Will didn't want to answer Rachel. But he knew his mum had gone into town and was dragging his dad out to the doctor's this afternoon to discuss their crazy son.

"Not long, I suppose," he said.

"So they'll find him and make sure he's OK?" she insisted.

"Yes, they'll be back soon! So now let's get out of here."

He laid the sticky knife on the floor in the back beside empty water bottles and a car repair manual. He started the engine and turned the van from the drive. And he didn't look back.

*

The ambulance in front slowed into Buttermere and pulled into the car park behind the pub. They all got out of their vehicles and gazed around them at how black the sky had become. The policemen could see the family waiting up on the hill. The father had already searched every individual stone and blade of grass in the little village, touched every door, laid his eyes on every open hole, but still, they could see, the mother hated him for not finding their daughter.

The paramedics took blankets up the hill to the family and the young policeman willed his breath to give him some strength.

He looked at the small gathering of people on the road and he felt sure, whether they would have the truth that day or not, that this particular mother was going to be given the words that would lodge in her head and not be moved; to be told what could only sound like a lie. And she would claw at every rock, every bush, every shard of ice scratching the lake, and she was going to deny until the very last that this death could even be possible.

The young officer went over Will's dad's tracks like more rain in shallow puddles. And over the exact stones Will had skimmed his feet over as he walked and then ran.

Leaking energy, drained already by the words he had had to speak and a solemnity he had to perfect, he dragged his feet through the grass in the fields. He would not be the one to find her. Could not be. He watched the snow-bumped earth in front of him and he managed his feet so as not to stumble. His eyes stayed away from the lake. Couldn't stand to stare into the frozen water, expecting any minute to see a waft of hair sail under the ice.

The field was safer, as it was much less likely to be hiding a death: at the worst a daft kid with chattering teeth who'd run from an argument and now felt it impossible to go back of her own free will. But they all seemed to know that wasn't going to be the case.

So he started to head back towards the family perched on the brow of the hill. The paramedics had tried to persuade them to come down to the pub car park where the ambulance was waiting, but they were still up on the road by the chapel.

One of them, the youngest, was strangely silent. As if his tongue had frozen like the water running from the drains behind the pub. And the policeman was worried that his older partner, raging internally at the idea of the dead child, would try to chip away roughly at the icicles that had frozen the brother and only make things worse.

When he eventually returned to meet his colleague's eye, they both shook their heads at each other like woeful dogs.

"I've spoken to the family," the senior one said. "And the dad won't hear of it. He's convinced she's round here somewhere. Says his lad wouldn't let anything happen to the girl, wouldn't have harmed a hair on her body, what they all say..."

The younger policeman could feel his face, greyer by the second, sagging from his bones. Old. Though he was only twenty-six.

"Bollocks to that," he replied. "We've no choice. We can't leave it till it's dark. Call the divers. The mother will agree anyway. She'll talk the dad round, or we will. You call them, and I'll go back up and smooth it over."

He saw his partner's eyes begin to bleed with resignation, his

172

fingers eager to get back home tonight and play with his kids. The younger officer turned back towards the track, where the village opened and the family stood up on the hill, the mother ready with a howl when she saw his blank face.

The divers waded into the lake and dunked their eel black bodies in the water. The two policemen stood by the trees, and the paramedics, waiting to load their stretcher with the thin weight of a girl, held onto more blankets. Eventually the mother had come down to wait behind the emergency workers, and the two sons had got into the police car on the hill with the dad. But now he was sitting on the side of the road, torn inside, with no idea what to lend his body or his mind to. The policemen saw him, but they had no news, and there was nothing they could say to put him at ease, so they left him alone in his confusion while they waited by the lake.

The policemen watched as the divers came up. Felt underneath their skin that they knew already what was about to happen. The officer whose mind was playing with the smile on the faces of his own children, and the way their arms looked in sleep, turned away. The younger one took the cold air into his lungs and found himself, after all, reaching forward towards the water, his shoes becoming islands at the edge of the lake. He grasped at the slippery arms that were heaved out to him. Felt the frozen flesh. Cold blood now static inside her. Turned his face away from the blue, blank, beautiful girl. Lifted. Took all the weight from the divers. And then she was on the pebble-covered shore. The mother rushing. The paramedics busy with the mother, holding her, and moving swiftly with the blankets to the dead girl.

The mother would have to identify this girl. He knew it. Even though it was hardly necessary and the way she was wailing said more than any nod of her head or a choked word could ever say.

Still, the policeman knew, he would have to ask her to confirm this. His hands were wet from the drowned girl, the sensation of watery skin that he thought he would never get rid of. He wiped them down on his trousers and turned as he felt his partner looking at him.

So he took another breath, glanced again at the drenched mouth, the swollen cheeks of the girl, and prepared to ask the mother if this was her daughter before the paramedics covered over the girl's face with the blanket, and wheeled her into the ambulance away from her life; officially into her deep death for good.

*

They hadn't gone far before Will pulled over.

Rachel watched him and thought it was catching him up. She put her hand on his arm.

"I can't do it," he said. "I think you'll have to drive."

"Will, we don't have to. We can turn around, go back and—"

"No, no, I can't go back," he said. "Not now, not ever. And I need to see it. Buttermere. Where she died." He stretched his arms out, his hands still grasping the steering wheel. "You'll have to drive, Rachel," he said.

She imagined her own feet for a moment, tense on the pedals, the van wobbling beneath her over the stone-splattered roads. And her hands trying desperately to keep control. It was years since she'd driven.

Rachel slid over Will on the seat, having to sit for a second on his knee, then shifting herself into position, touching the keys and the wheel as if negotiating her way around skin and bones she'd never encountered before. A new body under her fingers.

"Will, were you trying to...? To kill him?"

Will didn't answer. Didn't look at her.

You do realise how this all looks, don't you? You do understand what could happen?"

Will shrugged. "They'll all blame me. Of course they will, they always do. I know that."

"But... depending on what Martin says," Rachel spoke carefully, "they'll think you tried to kill him. Attempted murder, Will. That's how it looks."

She watched the words sink into him, then she turned the key and drove on.

"Then we'll have to turn our mobiles off," he said after a while. "Maybe throw them away."

"Why?" she asked. "I mean what if we break down or something?"

"No, don't you see? The police can trace you from your phone. We have to switch them off and get as far away as possible."

They took the same road into Buttermere as Will's dad had taken years before. Away from towns, shops, motorway, people. Up. Up, as if driving *into* the rocky hills.

Will had not been in the church for long. Asleep on a pew with a prayer mat under his cold head. Or was he only pretending to sleep? Martin had walked in and didn't see Will. Will is wondering just where Martin thought Will was: he knew he was no longer with the others at the lake. Maybe he thought Will had more sense and he'd slipped into the pub and tagged onto a group of ramblers to warm his toes by the fire. More likely that he didn't give Will a thought.

Martin crept into the church and walked up the aisle. He stopped and touched the face of the soldier on the wall. Let his hands drift over the brass cheeks, the nose, the tin helmet, as if he was delicately caressing skin. His fingertips lingering while his body moved on. Then he went up to the altar and Will could hear him sob. A strange noise to come from Will's brother. A noise he'd never heard before. In between each gulp, each drip of tears, Will realised Martin was speaking, repeating over and over again, forgive me. Oh God, forgive me.

Will was just waking up as they approached the tiny swell of Buttermere village, and the sight of the church sent his memory bank even further into overload.

They parked. Will's body was numb as he got out of the van beside walkers and tourists, while Rachel simply felt the relief of being able to stretch her legs. They went straight down to the lake.

The fields at either side of the track that led down there were swaying with yellow grass. And the hills behind the lake were like great, docile bumps in the earth. Everything seemed so calm, so serene. They could see the ridge between the two hills beyond the lake where hikers could pass from this pool of water to another without the heave of the roads.

At the lake the trees dipped their branches over in a tattered arc, almost touching the cool water; water that seemed to be lapping like a gentle sea onto the pebbly bay, instead of frozen still like before. It seemed to whisper, as the sun shining upon it followed the ripples on the surface. He could watch it for hours and try to follow the pattern, its shape, the rhythmic shimmy.

They sat down on the ground together at the side of the lake and Rachel asked Will if he wanted to be left alone at all to think about Theresa, maybe say a few words, maybe pray. He didn't. He said, with just a hint of embarrassment, that he never wanted to be left alone again.

The water was so shallow. The edges of it were nothing but a trickle. Is it true that you can drown in such shallow water?

He picked at pebbles and stones, and took some out of the cool water as if panning for gold. One bright white stone was left in his palm. Like an old perfectly preserved fossil. A pure bone. A secret.

"Well?" Rachel asked. "Do you remember it now? Do you know what happened?"

"Let's go into the chapel," he said.

Inside the church the cold was seriously getting to Will. He told himself over and over. Pitied himself for his chattering teeth, the deathly cold all over his body. And he lay down.

Where had Martin gone after that? He hadn't dreamt it, he's sure. Martin came into the church. Will pretended to be asleep so he could deny what he had just seen. In case Martin spotted him lying on the pews, he closed his eyes and made his face into a mask of sleep, until he really was asleep, and then when Will opened his eyes again Martin was gone; only Will's mum and dad, and their fear, were there.

Then the police and everybody seemed to bring their blame and hang it around Will's neck. He looked around. He was still, stupidly, looking for Theresa. Where was she? It was a joke, right? Some kind of sick joke. Martin was always doing things like this. Martin would have thought it was funny.

But when Will's eyes finally landed on Martin, he looked serious, leaning against the police car, identical blanket dozing on his shoulders, a cup of something hot in his hands, and he was telling them how he'd stayed in the car. He couldn't possibly have seen anything. He'd stayed there and then he'd walked up to the pub with the real fire and the busy bar, and he'd bought a pint. The landlord would confirm it. Will knew that was not the only building he'd been in, but he was too shocked and too scared to say anything.

It was as if that soldier had spoken to him. In clear words that brass cannot speak. If you go now, you can drag someone to safety like a soldier saving someone in the battle.

But Will was too cold. Had just escaped from that freezing wasteland of a stupid place to come for a holiday. So he ignored the prompting of this soldier, even though it seemed to plead with him, until it went limply silent. A brass engraving can't really speak to you, can it? He did not want to go back out there for anything. Not even if his life depended on it.

But what if he had known Theresa's life depended on it?

Will and Rachel walked up to the little chapel. He touched the iron gates before the entrance, with a plunge in his stomach. Rachel and Will went inside together. It was empty, apart from a collection plate on a table behind the door with a few scattered coins in it.

Rachel started going through her pockets for some change, while Will walked to the front of the church where the big Bible was still laid open on a stand. He sat down in one of the pews and touched the prayer mat in front of him. He'd used it as a pillow once.

What was he going to do now he had remembered Martin was there?

Will stood up suddenly. "Rachel," he said.

She turned. "Yeah?"

"I'm just..." he said. "I'm going back outside."

Rachel followed him as he went to the gates outside the door again and looked down over the lake and the valley. He could see the pub where Martin must have gone afterwards to drink his pint that day, and the road here by the chapel where the police cars had waited.

His mum had gone to the lake with the police and the

paramedics while Will, Martin and their dad had sat in one of the cars. And then their dad had got out, impatient for news, and Martin had leaned over and gripped Will's shoulder hard.

"What did you see?' he hissed.

"What are you talking about?'

"Theresa. Did you see her?"

"No, I was asleep... I was cold... I went to the chapel..."

"What else did you see?"

Will was silent. Scared. He would use all the strength he had to deny everything. He would forget what he had seen in the chapel.

"Why didn't you do something?" Martin had demanded, with the same urgency but without the panic left in his voice.

Will had looked at his brother sitting with him in the police car. It was in Will's eyes. He could feel it. Fear. He was sure Martin could see he was scared. Then Martin let go of his shoulder and gave it a little shove.

He shrugged. "Shit happens, Will," he said. "Accidents happen. But I know as well as you do that you abandoned her. There's some legal jargon for not helping someone when you can save them. I'd keep that quiet if I were you. And if you don't tell anyone, I won't either. But just remember, I can drop you in it the moment I want to."

*

"What are we going to do?"

We are going to live.

Rachel, used to the van now, drove some more. They circled back around the water, caught the sloping side of Keswick and joined the M6, running dangerously close to their village again. They swooped past it, both silent in the cabin. On the motorway Rachel became scared for a while and they stopped at a service

179

station where they ate plastic sandwiches for lunch and drank coffee from paper cups.

She had to turn her phone on to get the address they were going to, so she checked it secretly while Will went to the toilet and had turned it off by the time he came back and found her staring at its blank face. "Do you think the police can track us even when our phones are turned off?" she asked, as she slipped it back in her pocket and followed Will out to the van again. Maybe Will didn't hear her.

The road to Manchester became full of doubt the closer they got. Will, driving again now, cursed at every wrong turn they took.

"Do you even know where it is?" he asked Rachel.

There were lots of things she'd left behind in her little terraced house. She'd already told him there were things she would have brought if she'd had time, if she'd known they were going to be running away.

She was sure she had an A-Z of Manchester, that her dad had once sent her out of the blue, as if he was suddenly feeling the pangs of not knowing his own daughter. But it was still in the house with all her other things, still sitting with the house dust and the swirling memory of Rachel's gran and granddad.

She said she knew vaguely which part of Manchester it was and they slowed by pavements to ask the curled away faces of people on the street for directions.

Eventually they got there. Rachel knocked at the wrong house and was shown down three doors until she came to the right one. No idea what she would say, she put her fist up to the door and banged out her arrival.

"Rachel? My God, Rachel?"

"Hello dad." She marked a spot in her brain that flinched at how much older he looked. "Can we come in?"

He opened the door wide and stepped back to let them in. He only seemed to register the existence of Will once he had taken in, processed, and accepted the fact that his daughter was here.

"This is Will," Rachel said. "My... He's my... we are..."

Her dad nodded and held out his hand to Will. "Pleased to meet you," he said. "Well, this is a surprise, Rachel. Why didn't you let me know you were coming?" He was forcing some kind of normality between his words, bridging each gap between syllables with a laid back easiness. She was his daughter, after all. Why shouldn't she come and see him?

"It's complicated, dad. I didn't really know myself, not until we were on our way."

"Well, you're here now. It's been a long time. Things have..." Keith's words trailed in the air as he walked away from the doorway where Rachel and Will were still standing. Rachel glanced at Will and saw his head down, staring at the ground. She felt how fragile his peace was. That any one aspect of the peace he now seemed to have could slip away again at any time.

She called after her dad who'd gone through to the kitchen and was getting ready to offer them a drink. "Where's mum?" Rachel said, and then she turned and whispered to Will's bent head, "Are you OK? Do you need to sit down or something?"

Keith was walking back towards Rachel and he caught her whisper as it breathed into Will's face. He looked at the pair of them. Seemed to smell the fright.

"Are you two in some kind of trouble?" he asked.

"Why?"

"Just asking, Rachel. You turn up unannounced after we haven't seen each other in... how long is it?" He shrugged. "Of course, I'm not saying I'm not glad to see you, but, well, why now? And then there's this lad here, looks like he's just been pulled from the bloody trenches. Are you all right, lad?" Keith peered at Will's bent head, his hands shoved deep down in his pockets, his shoulders hunched around his neck. "You know, Rachel," Keith said, "I've been in enough trouble myself through the years to recognise a dose of it when it's standing in my own hallway. Why don't you two come and sit down and tell me what's going on."

Martin's blood is still staining Rachel's mind as she follows her dad to this unknown kitchen. She feels the weight of the loneliness in the air, her subconscious has already sensed the separation. She thinks that everybody is always alone when it matters. It's harsh. Because nobody would want to be left to die all on their own, with no hand, no voice, no comfort. She stops and lets her dad walk on ahead out of earshot and takes her phone from her pocket. She looks at Will, "I have to know," she says.

"What? What are you doing?"

"I can't just leave it like that. I have to know he's OK."

"Martin? You're thinking about Martin?"

"It isn't because it's him. You mustn't think that, Will. I just can't leave someone to bleed to death. I don't care who he is or what he's done. I just can't."

"Then at least go and use a phone box! You can't call from here. They will trace it right back to this address!"

Rachel left Will with her dad and eventually found a phone box. But there was no answer.

*

Cath hadn't persuaded the doctor that Will needed to be sectioned, but she was already planning to go back to the senior partner for a second opinion. So Ian had spent the whole journey home telling her to leave it at that and not to bother the doctors any more. It was a waste of their time. It was a waste of his time too, he'd taken a half day so he could go to the doctor's with her after lunch.

But when they got home Ian forgot all about that. He stared at the signs of chaos inside the house and wondered if this time Cath might be right.

Martin had been clever. He'd understood the signs of shock and had pulled himself to his knees and walked on them till he got to the hallway, where he'd dragged his mum's long winter coat down from the rack and wrapped it around his shoulders awkwardly. Then he'd knee-walked back into the living room and leaned himself against the sofa where he'd stayed until his mum and dad came home.

Cath felt the fizz of trouble in the air as soon as she walked into the house. Then she found Martin in front of the sofa. When he summoned up an effort to peel away her brown woollen coat and showed her the damage she held her hand to her mouth.

"I told you," she gasped to Ian. "I knew something like this would happen. He's done it this time."

Then she unfolded her ruined coat from Martin's arms and said, "Are you going to be OK? Ian, call an ambulance! What happened to you?!"

Martin only shook his head and could hardly speak.

"It wasn't Will..." he managed.

No, it wasn't Will's fault, he thought to himself. It was that bitch of a woman who'd poisoned his brain and coloured his blood.

"What did he do to you?" she yelled, almost screaming the house down.

Martin winced.

"It wasn't his fault," he insisted. No, Will would only do whatever she wanted him to do.

Cath blew angry air from her mouth. "Of course it's his bloody fault," she said.

Between them, Cath and Ian managed to get Martin to sit up and Cath looked at the cloth Rachel had roughly dressed the wounds with. Martin pulled at it and said he didn't want anything *she'd* put there.

Cath tried to stop him, but it wasn't really holding back the blood any more: if it ever had done.

She had been the cause of this, he told himself. Will had been gentle and docile until she came on the scene. He'd gone along with everything Martin wanted. Still would do if Rachel hadn't come along and ruined everything.

"It was that bitch Rachel," Martin cried out through the pain.

"Relax, Martin," said Ian, pressing a large lump of cotton wool into the deep indent in his son's muscly shoulder. He pressed a clean bandage in place. "Just hold on a bit longer, the ambulance is on its way."

Ruined everything.

"All women are like that," he stuttered. They had taken his friends away from wanting to spend so many nights in the pub as lads together: had reduced grown men into wimps pampering to their every need.

Cath didn't know what to make of that, silenced.

And until that bitch Rachel came along he had Will where he wanted him. *She* had injected some spark back into him. Had now delved into Will's memories and brought back up what had been safely hidden there.

"They ruin everything," he whispered.

Cath flinched, and recovered from her speechlessness. "I know you don't mean that, Martin love. I know you're in shock. But not all women are like Rachel and one day you'll find—"

"Don't, for God's sake, tell me I'll find someone," Martin said, summoning strength he didn't know he had. "Why the hell would I want to do that? I've only got to look at you and how you've drained dad to know I never want that. You're all the same. Bitches. Bloody bitches. Rachel, you, Theresa."

Cath held back the tears, trying to push away the glimmer of truth she'd seen in her son's eyes. Denied it, so she would soon be able to forget that she had ever seen it at all.

"You'll feel better when we get you to the hospital," she whispered gently, hoarse with imminent tears. "The ambulance will be here soon."

And she went to the phone to call the police but broke down in tears before she could dial the first 9.

*

"Isn't it a little bit early?" Rachel asked, coming back with no word from the phone box to find Keith plunging a blackened corkscrew into a cheap bottle of wine.

Keith looked at his watch. "Is it?" he said. "Well, I thought you two looked as if you could do with it."

He poured the wine and then sat at the table with Will and Rachel. "So, what's going on?" he asked.

Rachel took Will's hand. "There has been a bit of trouble," she said. "I don't really know where to start. But..." Rachel looked around her at the unwashed pots in the kitchen sink and the opened loaf of bread, sprung like a jack-in-a-box by the pot drainer. And she realised the reason for the coldness in the room. "Where's mum?" Rachel asked slowly. "What time will she be back?"

"Your mum—" he began.

"Where has she gone? What happened?"

But Rachel didn't know whether to feel pity or anger at this man for losing the one thing he had held onto so far.

"I'm afraid I don't know," he said. "Your mum has left me, Rachel. The truth is, I've no idea where she's gone."

*

There was a commotion up on the hill when Andrea arrived back in the village after her years of searching for an elusive future. She could see the blue lights swinging in the misty air, like a tiny version of the Blackpool illuminations – as if she had brought them with her.

She was too worried about whether Rachel would have changed the locks to pay much attention at first and then she was swallowed up by tidying and cleaning, to surprise Rachel when she got home from work.

Forgot all about the commotion, until her stomach realised it would soon be dinner time, and she heard all about it in the queue at the butcher's. The whisper travelled down the line of people, even wafting out into the air around the door.

"Well, it's obvious, isn't it? It must have been him. That lad was always a bit strange. I mean, all that business with that sister of his, you know. Before they even lived here that was."

"So did the ambulance get to the hospital in time?"

"Was it definitely the brother? I know he's gone missing like, but do they know it was him that done it?"

Andrea shifted uncomfortably, counting the slabs of steak on the tray and watching the looped sausage curl like clasped fingers.

"That's what I heard," another woman was saying. "Who else could it have been? After that business with *her,* you know, *losing the baby and everything,*" she whispered. "And she's old enough to be... well, the lad went... not surprising I suppose. If that girl's grandmother was alive today... carrying on like that."

It *was* Rachel they were talking about. Andrea felt the back of her neck begin to itch, her face feel uncomfortable. The girl's *grandmother*. Had Andrea been away for so long that no one in the village even knew she existed? She didn't recognise any of them: she wondered if they were all intruders who had taken over the village with the new housing developments.

What a bad time the girl had had lately, they said. Got involved with the wrong lad, much younger than her, got pregnant — Andrea paused in her listening and began the unstoppable thought of a baby — suffered a miscarriage... and Andrea felt the presence of the child somehow, never seen, never heard.

Was this what she had come back to? Overhearing all about her daughter through gossip in the butcher's.

"Yes," the woman in the queue in front of Andrea was saying. "It's as much her fault as it is his. And she's gone missing too. Why didn't *she* stop him or at least fetch help? No, as guilty as he is, I call her. You wouldn't have stood by and watched that going on, would you?"

Andrea was frozen, listening.

"What did he ever do to deserve that, poor love."

The gossip in the queue went on. "Poor Martin. Even if he survives, he'll never be the same, you know."

Never be the same.

One of the women looked up and caught Andrea's eye. A flash of recognition and the woman went quiet. It couldn't be long, Andrea thought, before they all realised who she was. Andrea turned around and left the shop, pushing past the last few customers in the queue. Couldn't stand all that gossip when it affected her. Wasn't hungry any more anyway.

She had finally left Keith when she realised that her life with him was never going to reach the likes of those sky-touching first moments in Blackpool ever again. It had all been downhill since that day. But she'd clung onto it for so long. Was that love? Not giving up, was that what it meant?

As she walked alone in her thoughts she saw her whole life was almost identical to Mary's after all, and squirmed and winced and ran.

*

"You don't know where mum is?" Rachel asked again when Will had gone through to watch TV. "No idea at all?"

Keith shook his head. Lifted the wineglass to his mouth. Drank.

Oh God, here it is, Rachel thought. This is his new lie. So he doesn't hide his head in fruit machines and horse racing any more. This is what he does now.

She watched his face, his skin hardened and deeply lined, his eyes struggling to keep up with the change from night to day, and in a place at the core of her dad's own being, with a centrality she despised, Rachel saw her previous self. Running. Searching. All those months. All those men. She knew what she had been looking for, what she was still desperate to confirm she would find in Will. What was her dad running from? Was he looking for the same love, of someone he could rely on?

"She always wanted more, you know, your mum."

"What?"

"I was never enough really," Keith said. "Life was never enough. She always wanted more. You should just be happy, don't you think? After all, there isn't anything more."

Rachel nodded slowly. "Suppose," she said. She took a drink, and she could see how the same weaknesses in herself might have made her turn out like that too. She sees the possibility of it in the way their faces move so alike one another, the way they both clutch. And yet she knows she has refused to become like him: always an addict to something.

She had remained hardened to it. Decided a long time ago, that she simply would not become so sad and desperate. But what was she doing instead? Wasn't she just as desperate to feel loved? Was she crazy to stay with Will after what he had done? Would he stand by her if she had done the same thing?

She'd always ached to find the kind of love her gran and granddad had. She'd watched them together, seamless every day, and she'd thought that would be all she'd ever need. A love like that. She hoped with all her heart that she'd found it in Will. And she would do all she possibly could to make sure she had.

But it didn't feel how she expected it to. It was a different colour. An unusual shape. It wasn't drawn in the same way as Mary and Arthur's had been.

"What kind of trouble are you in, Rachel?" Keith asked. "Why have you really come?"

She thought about Martin and his blood, couldn't get rid of that thought, and about Will sitting in the other room, waiting for her to betray him. And she knew that what had happened between the two brothers and even Will's trauma over his sister's death were small things to her personally, just slight dents in happiness. And the thing that could make her run and run was as big as a comet. The loss she hadn't had a chance to grieve for.

"I was pregnant," she said.

Her dad looked up from his glass in alarm.

"But I lost it." She shrugged and felt tears begin deep in her throat. "See," she said. "I couldn't even keep that with me. I can't seem to hang onto anything."

Keith took her hand on the table and shushed her gently in an amazing, perfect tone. "What are you talking about, can't hang on to anything?" he said. "That wasn't your fault, and I'd say you're hanging onto something pretty well." He jerked his head towards the other room. "How old is that lad?" he asked. "And he's still with you. He stuck around even after that."

"Yes but… it's not how I thought it would be, dad." she said.

"What's that?"

"Oh, you know, life. Love. I used to look at gran and granddad and think that was how it would be. That's what love looks like. But mine doesn't look like that. Mine isn't like that at all."

"Oh Rachel," Keith said. "You're just remembering what you want to remember. And you're forgetting the stuff that doesn't suit you. Your gran only got married because she was pregnant, same as your mum, and your granddad only married her because he had to, same as me."

"Dad! That can't be…"

Keith shrugged. "Sounds awful, I know," he said. "But it's true. If Mary hadn't been pregnant she wouldn't have got married when she did, and then who knows what would have happened, maybe she wouldn't have married Arthur Barnes at all."

He took another swig of wine and then poured more into his empty glass. Rachel was wondering why he bothered with the dainty little glass at all.

"Same as me and your mum, love." he said. "Now that's one thing you can say for yourself, you're not with that lad because you have to be, are you? You're with him because you want to be. And anyway, who says love has to look a certain way? Mary and Arthur never stopped bloody bickering as far as I can remember."

At the end of the bed Ian moved awkwardly from one foot to the other.

"Martin, how long are you going to go on like this, refusing to talk to your mum?"

Martin's wound had been stitched and dressed while the drugs now kept him still.

"She's concerned about you, you must realise that. And you're just making it worse."

Martin couldn't move, and still felt a dull ache somewhere below the numbness of the painkillers. His stitches were tight and the dressing was pulling on his skin. Otherwise he would have walked away from his dad, and all these questions, there and then.

"She just wants to know if Will did it or—"

"None of her bloody business."

"Well, you did say it was all her fault," Ian said. "So was it—?"

"Just shut up dad and leave me alone! You think I was stabbed by a girl?!"

Will said he didn't want Rachel to use a phone box anywhere near her dad's house if she insisted on calling to check on Martin. So she persuaded him to take her in the van; after all, she'd had to walk for ages to find one in the first place: if there had been any phone boxes in the area her dad lived in they wouldn't have remained working for long.

No answer. Rachel would wait, and keep trying again.

Will stayed in the van. He definitely didn't want to hear the conversation when she got through.

Will thought about being in the church, when Martin came in. He thought about before that, leaving Theresa there by the lake with his mum and dad because he hated the cold and hated being there, and he hated the insistent feeling that he was being made to do this. He wasn't a child anymore. They couldn't make him trudge pointlessly round a crappy lake in the freezing cold if he didn't want to.

Martin had refused, walkman still on, when they got there. They had let him stay in the car and he wasn't that much older than Will: he said there was no way he was walking around in the freezing cold. Just what Will wanted to say, but couldn't.

Whether Will liked it or not, he was in the middle, between his little sister and his older brother. But once he had started around the lake he couldn't stand it any longer. He wasn't a child any more. He wasn't responsible for his sister, it couldn't go on like that. Wanted to only do what he wanted to do. So Will had simply walked away, heading for the car where Martin was supposed to be waiting.

Will had not stopped when he noticed Martin pass him going the other way. He was going to shout after him, warn him about the waste of time, the big, dull lake, - "Don't bother! There's nothing there!" - but he just kept his head down and walked.

Even so something made him feel uneasy, so then he turned and followed his brother at a distance. He was about to leave him to it: Martin looked as if he was going to walk round the stupid bloody lake after all. But then in the distance Will saw Theresa coming back along the path on her own: looking for him!

But Will wasn't just playing hide-and-seek to amuse her, he truly didn't want to be found: she would only persuade him to start off round the lake again.

As he hid, he saw Martin also sneak under the branches of an overhanging tree, but he knew he was going to make her jump, frighten the life out of her. And he thought about how Martin was always doing things like that to Theresa. How he goaded her and teased her and how Will had sometimes thought one day it would go too far.

Will was about to shout through the silent sky to stop the prank from happening, but he was cold, and he didn't want to give away that he was there. He wanted to find somewhere warm.

Leave Martin to walk around the stupid lake with Theresa instead. Let him do something for once.

So he turned back towards the car park and ran.

But the truth is more vivid than lies.

Martin leapt out behind Theresa as she walked past. Made her jump quickly. Too quickly. She slipped on the icy ground by the water and went in.

Gasping with the cold plunge, her clothes drenched by the lake, she held her hand up towards Martin for help. Martin took it roughly but then toyed with her, letting go so she slid back into the water with a squeal.

Had Will heard that cry for help in real life? Does he even remember hearing the distant squawk of what he assumed to be a cold and hungry bird?

But Martin bent down and held her head under the water for a few moments. Sneered as he let her come up gasping for breath, and then repeated his bullying again and again, a little longer each time, strangely relishing the sight of the bewildered face that stared into his eyes when it came up for air. Was energised by the power it gave him, until suddenly she had stopped struggling, and he hurriedly shoved her and kicked her back into the water. Saw her drift out of sight under a patch of ice. And ran.

*

Rachel had rehearsed in her head what she would say if Martin picked up the phone, dizzied by the loss of blood, angry and maybe only able to whisper as the last of his breath slipped away from him.

Worse still, she thought through the words she would utter if Cath answered. She probably had the police tracing the call and would tear them limb from limb when they were found. Will was right that they would have to abandon the van soon; it was only a matter of time before the police would track it down.

"Hello?"

"Is that...? Sorry, is that Ian?"

"Rachel?"

"Yeah, look, I know what you must think, but really Will didn't mean... he didn't... how's Martin? Is he OK?"

"He's at the hospital with his mum now. I've just come home for his stuff."

Ian had been lingering in the house trying to hide from it all, trying to work out a way to push all this horror from his brain, when the phone on the wall by the spindle banister had rung.

Rachel could hear the confusion in his voice, the dipping under each word that came from not understanding how these things had happened to his family. How did a family get like this?

"The doctors say he'll be all right. But he's in shock, saying some funny things... what happened here anyway?"

But Rachel knew she wasn't the one to give him the answers he was looking for. Knew nothing about families, after all.

She put the phone down. There was a crack on the other end as she took the receiver away from her ear, Ian's voice only a quiver.

Will looked white when she woke him up. But she made him get out of the van, walk calmly around the corner, and then they ran. Back to her dad's house.

*

Will had always insisted he remembered being born. He described the birth canal, the muffled sounds of life and the squeeze of his shoulders as he pushed himself forward. A desperate fight, a struggle to get out, begin life. Nobody believed him – his dad flipped the ridiculous notion away, his mum, finding each of the three births were reduced down to a revolving mass of pain and a subsequent loathing of her own body, pushed

194

away the idea that anybody would wish to remember such a thing.

Only Will's sister, who wasn't too sure, even dared to imagine for a single moment that there could be any truth in Will's claim.

Sometimes Theresa thought Will was exaggerating, but she believed everything he told her. He knew that. He could have told her the petals on the pansies in the garden were the spare wings of butterflies, only used on special occasions. Or that when the breeze shook the trees it was really a sort of language, one tree communicating with another. And Theresa would have smiled and nodded. Taken the information into her heart.

If he had told her Martin was going to kill her, she would have believed him. But how was he to have known? He now realised Martin was obviously jealous of the attention Will gave her, but he couldn't know he would do *that*.

All he cared about was what Theresa would think, if she was here. Would she think he had let her down when she needed him most?

There was nothing he could actually do now. Martin would continue to deny any knowledge of what happened, and Cath wouldn't believe Will if he told her.

But what would Theresa say to him, he wondered. What would she do?

She would stick by Will. She would believe in him. Give him another chance. He knew that. And there was only other person in the world who would do all that. He wasn't going to let her go as well.

*

There was no dawn raid on Keith's house to find the fugitives. But Rachel and Will didn't go out all day, just to be safe. It appeared to be no hardship for Will, as he stayed in front of the television all afternoon, while Keith made beans on toast for lunch and opened another bottle.

Keith turned to Rachel as she was doing the washing-up. "I'm sorry," he said.

"What for?"

"For leaving you there with Mary and Arthur all those years ago. You were too young. It was unforgivable."

And Rachel shook her head. "Don't be silly." she said. "I wouldn't change it. It was the best thing. I can't imagine what it would have been like to live with you and mum then. And anyway," she said, "gran taught me a lot. Important things."

"Oh yeah, like what?"

"Like, how to hold out for the right person."

"Oh that."

"Yeah, she told me not to give my heart away too quickly. And I never did. I waited until I found the right one."

Keith took his daughter awkwardly in his arms. "Have you?"

She smiled at him. "I think so," she said.

"You certainly look like a couple," Keith went on. "You look right together. I can imagine you two with that baby. Will you try again, do you think?" he asked. "For a baby. Will you let me know?"

But Rachel smiled and shook her head. "Nah," she said. "Can you imagine me as a mother?"

During her second lonely evening in the house, when Rachel still didn't come home, the neighbours came to the door to offer their knowledge to Andrea.

"So where is she now?" Andrea asked.

Her neighbours shook their heads. "Gone off," they said. "With the lad, we presume, since he's disappeared as well."

But Andrea saw in their faces that they couldn't feel the weight of their own words at all.

"Stabbed his own brother, you know."

"They won't let him out of hospital yet. He won't be the same, if you ask me." And then the whisper. "There's something *different* about him now. Something not quite right. Do you know, he wouldn't have the police, wouldn't press charges or let them go looking for that brother of his or anything. Can you imagine it? No police, even after being attacked like that for no reason. Now that's family loyalty gone too far if you ask me."

And there was a woman from the same village who was also feeling as if she had lost her family for ever. Another woman, wishing she could strip it all back and become again what she once was. A woman on her own in the hospital, whose children had all been taken away in one way or another.

The truth was itching at Cath's body as she remembered her son's last words to her. Martin had shouted after her as she sat in tears by the phone in the hall, "No police. I mean it. You call the police and I'll bloody kill you."

*

They are lying in bed in the little terrace house they are renting. Will has just got back from the swimming baths. He looks invigorated and refreshed from his efforts with the water. He still has the redness in his hair, and whenever his stubbly chin verges on a beard, it's pure ginger. Rachel resists the urge to ruffle it, like a mother would. She hates the steps of maternity that still creep inside her.

They'd lived with Keith for two weeks and Rachel said it was enough. He understood how she felt. Felt the same way about himself.

But he shook Will's hand as they stood in the doorway, the new key poised in Will's fingers. Keith thought it was probably the closest he would ever get to giving his daughter away. And he felt glad of being able to do that.

"I'm going to have to change my number," he says flatly.

"So," Rachel says, "you're still not going to reply?"

Will shakes his head. "No," he says. "No chance. Martin can send me as many messages as he likes. I won't be receiving them."

"What did he say this time?"

"He says he's going to move out," Will says. "He hasn't spoken to mum since the day he went to hospital. But he says I owe him one now because he didn't go to the police. Can you believe that? After what he did!"

"Will," she says gently. "You weren't trying to kill him, were you...?"

"No, Rachel, of course I wasn't." The emotion of the moment revisits him briefly. "But I just felt I had to shut him up somehow."

"So what are you going to do now?"

"All I have to do is change my number. That will shut him up for ever. I'll never need to tell anyone how much I know; *him*, my mum and dad, the police... I mean, what good would it do anyway? It's one thing me remembering what happened in Buttermere, and how Theresa... died. But now I'm getting on with my life. And you're my family now, not them. Not after the way they treated me. I've made up my mind."

Before Will and Rachel, a bunch of students lived here. They left a hole just the size of a fist in the wall between the two bedrooms, a toilet with no seat that's clay brown in the bowl, and mould in the kitchen and inside each chipped china mug, but Will and Rachel don't care. They lie in silence for a moment.

Will cannot see her face but he can feel Rachel trying to hold back a smile. She is going to ask the question again.

"Will."

"Yep?"

She takes his hand and moves it to her body.

"Are you going to call your mum, Will?"

He doesn't answer, but Rachel can feel his smile begin to break into a short laugh.

"You don't have to speak to Martin. But don't you think your mum should know about us? Where we live – what if she needed you for something?"

He knows the script now. He knows she doesn't really want to share their joint life with his parents. Even though there would be something satisfying about proving Cath wrong. *Look at us, we made it.*

He smiles. "I'll make you a deal," he says. "I'll speak to mine if you speak to yours."

And he knows how she will answer. He feels he knows every answer she has inside her. He knows the words by heart now. It is the truth looped between the words that makes his mouth open and his breath catch on his tongue. He waits, feeling it build.

"You've got to be joking," she says. "Besides, I've got you, I don't need anyone else."

And they both believe it. She playfully hits his shoulder, and inside her, where neither she nor Will can feel or suspect yet, a tiny life kicks into action. An unseen chain reaction beginning. An unstoppable, un-plannable, irrational act.

"So we're agreed then?" he asks. "No family."

"Yeah," she says. "Who needs 'em?"

If you have enjoyed this book...

... you have proved there is still a place for new novelists.

Our Pioneer Readers series exists to provide opportunities for new fiction writers: publishing is becoming a harder and harder world to break into, unless you are already famous for something else!

So if you have enjoyed this book, think about buying copies as presents for other readers. You will help us increase the opportunities available to other new authors who can't get today's big publishers interested in their work.

We are looking for pioneer readers – readers who are willing to buy and read the books we publish.

We intend to publish the work of another new novelist each year, discovering creative writers who do not set out simply to replicate a publisher's formula... and there are more than enough authors out there with high-quality manuscripts! You can help them 'reveal their leaves to the world'.

So if you would be interested in becoming a pioneer reader and buying a discounted package of books to pass on to friends, visit us at:
www.pioneer-readers.org

Interested in short stories by new authors?
Full details of our short story publications are available on our website
www.5photostory.com

Want to give feedback to one of our authors?
We welcome constructive comments about all our titles, and invite you to share your feedback on our discussion board online at:
www.fygleaves.co.uk/discussionboard/index.php